City DOGS

Glenda Goertzen

Illustrated by Peter Hudecki

Fitzhenry & Whiteside

Published in Canada by Fitzhenry & Whiteside, 195 Allstate Parkway, Markham, Ontario L3R 4T8

Published in the United States by Fitzhenry & Whiteside, 311 Washington Street, Brighton, Massachusetts 02135

www.fitzhenry.ca   godwit@fitzhenry.ca

10 9 8 7 6 5 4 3 2 1

Library and Archives Canada Cataloguing in Publication

Goertzen, Glenda
    City dogs / Glenda Goertzen ; illustrated by Peter Hudecki.

ISBN-13: 978-1-55455-005-0   ISBN-10: 1-55455-005-X

    1. Dogs—Juvenile fiction. I. Hudecki, Peter II. Title.

PS8613.O37C58 2007   jC813'.6   C2006-906872-0

U.S. Publisher Cataloging-in-Publication Data
(Library of Congress Standards)
    Goertzen, Glenda.
    City dogs / Glenda Goertzen ; illustrated by Peter Hudecki.
[128] p. : ill. ; cm.
Summary: When Pierre and Dare are dognapped, their fellow Prairie Dogs follow them to the big city, where their old enemy Bull is waiting for them—and so are a host of new friends.
ISBN-10: 1-55455-005-X (pbk.) ISBN-13: 9781554550050 (pbk.)
1. Dogs – Fiction – Juvenile literature. I. Hudecki, Peter. II. Title.
[Fic] dc22 PZ7.S547 2007

Fitzhenry & Whiteside acknowledges with thanks the Canada Council for the Arts, and the Ontario Arts Council for their support of our publishing program. We acknowledge the financial support of the Government of Canada through the Book Publishing Industry Development Program (BPIDP) for our publishing activities.

Design by Fortunato Design Inc.
Printed in Canada

Praise for *The Prairie Dogs*

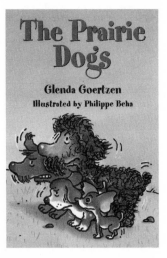

"More than just another fish-out-of-water story, this is a delightful, fast-paced tale of canine survival and camaraderie that ends with a wholly satisfying conclusion. An excellent choice for young fans of animal fiction."
—*Quill & Quire*

"The plot moves very well and keeps the reader's interest. The text is large and easy to read. The novel is highly recommended as a read aloud book to younger children and a must for school, public and personal libraries for middle year students."
—*Canadian Materials*

"Glenda Goertzen's novel, *The Prairie Dogs*, has moments of drama, and is lots of fun—a touching and absolutely delightful story!"
—*HI-RISE*

OLA Silver Birch Award shortlist, 2005

Saskatchewan Young Readers' Choice Diamond Willow Award shortlist, 2006

Table of Contents

Pierre

Mew

Old
Sam

Dare

Mouse

Bull

Chapter One
Old Enemies

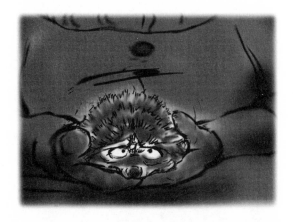

"OH NO, IT'S THAT LOONY ENGLISHMAN, Mr. Abram." Mrs. Schmeck cupped her hands protectively around the hedgehog sitting on her knee in the waiting room of the Silvertree Pet Clinic and Animal Shelter. "We'll be here all morning, listening to stories about his crazy dogs. And you'll have to treat their backsides for frostbite."

The vet's assistant crossed the waiting room and looked out the window to see what Mrs. Schmeck was talking about. Out of the swirling soup of snow came a man with a cane in one hand and four leashes in the other. The dogs were locked in sitting positions, forcing him to drag them along the icy front walk.

Mrs. Schmeck glared at the paintings on the walls of the waiting room. They had been donated to the clinic by the artist, Mr. Abram. Each painting featured a small dog. A black poodle did a flip in midair. A red terrier emerged from what seemed to be a burrow in a field of wildflowers. A hungry-looking Chihuahua chased a butterfly. A puppy tried to climb an elm tree. In the largest painting, the four small dogs were gathered around a sad-eyed basset hound. The little dogs looked cute and innocent, nothing like the unruly troublemakers Mrs. Schmeck knew them to be.

"There's nothing to be afraid of, you stubborn wagscallions!" Mr. Abram panted as he hauled his dogs through the front entrance. "It's just a check-up. Oh, hello, Mrs. Schmeck! Dare, please stop barking at that poor hedgehog! You'll have to forgive her, Mrs. Schmeck. She and the others were forced to spend a month here at the shelter over the summer, and she's never gotten over it. Did I ever tell you why I adopted them?"

"Yes, you did," Mrs. Schmeck said.

"I collapsed of a stroke at that old abandoned water park," Mr. Abram went on, "and these four courageous little strays gave up their freedom to go for help. They saved my life!"

"I know," Mrs. Schmeck said. "You tell everyone you meet."

Mr. Abram wiped the frost off his glasses and perched them on his nose. "Well, perhaps you haven't heard the story of how Pierre went over the wall of his kennel and started a riot, allowing nearly every dog in the shelter to escape!"

"Yes, I have," Mrs. Schmeck said. "Several times."

While the humans were talking, the feisty red terrier, Daredevil—Dare for short—was throwing suspicious growls at everyone in the room, even the hedgehog, which had rolled into a spiky ball. Pierre, a black miniature poodle with a friendly face and intelligent dark eyes, gave the terrier a reassuring bump with his nose. Mitzy, a young beagle cross, bounded across the room to get a closer look at Mr. Weibe's cat and took a tumble as she tripped over her own paws. Mitzy was in her "teenage" stage of growth, all legs and ears. She bounced to her feet and stood in front of the cat, tail wagging. Although the cat had hissed at the other dogs, it seemed quite friendly toward Mitzy.

The door to one of the examination rooms opened and Dr. Elbright appeared.

"There you are, Mr. Abram. Please bring the dogs in. Dr. Young will be with you shortly, Mrs. Schmeck."

Mrs. Schmeck grumbled something as Mr. Abram wrestled the dogs into the exam room. Dr. Elbright helped him lift Old Sam onto the steel table.

"I think that hound weighs more than I do," Mr. Abram gasped.

"Did you put him on the diet I suggested?" The vet stroked the basset hound. He gazed up at her with mournful eyes, as if he didn't expect to get out of the room alive.

"I did, but all he has to do is give the others a sad look and they let him eat their supper. No one can give a sad look like Old Sammy."

Dr. Elbright examined Old Sam, gave him his annual shots—the other dogs winced—and glanced at her chart. "Mr. Abram, I see only four dogs here. Isn't one missing?"

"Good lord, you're right. I've lost Mouse!" He was about to rush back outside when his coat gave a muffled yip. "Oh! I forgot."

He reached into his coat pocket and extracted a Chihuahua, which he placed on the floor. For a few moments the tiny dog bounced around cheerfully at the end of his leash. Then, realizing where he was, he froze, his enormous eyes bulging with terror.

"Be especially thorough when you examine Mouse, Dr. Elbright," said Mr. Abram. "When he's overexcited he has a habit of—whoops, there he goes."

The Chihuahua had fainted.

Dr. Elbright picked him up. "We noticed the fainting during Mouse's stay with us. We couldn't find anything wrong with him, so it's probably vasovagal syncope."

Mr. Abram gasped. "Is it serious?"

"No. It just means he faints when he's frightened."

Mouse's exam was easy, as he was unconscious for most of it, but Dare's was more of a challenge. It took both of the humans to wrestle her onto the table and calm her down. Dr. Elbright rolled Dare onto her back and gently prodded the terrier's belly. Dare growled.

"The dogs are filling out nicely, aren't they?" Mr. Abram patted Dare's head.

"Mr. Abram," the vet said, "Dare is not 'filling out.' She's pregnant!"

"Pregnant!" Mr. Abram sputtered. "How? I mean, are you sure?"

"Quite sure," Dr. Elbright said. "The due date can't be more than a week away."

"I thought she was just getting chubby. I myself always put on a few extra pounds in the winter—"

"Mr. Abram." Dr. Elbright tapped her foot. "Didn't I advise you when you adopted the dogs to have her spayed immediately? Do you have any idea how many unwanted puppies and kittens we receive every year?"

Mr. Abram snatched Dare away from the vet and cradled her protectively. "No puppy of my Dare would ever go unwanted!"

Dr. Elbright sighed and shook her head. Next she examined the father of the unborn puppies. Pierre was in excellent health and behaved very well for the exam, glancing in a superior way at the other dogs as if to show them how it was done.

When she examined Mitzy, the beagle cross, Dr. Elbright paid close attention to the young dog's throat and lungs. Mr. Abram claimed she sometimes made a "hissing" noise, but the vet could find nothing wrong with her.

As the dogs and the two humans left the room, the door to the other examination room swung open. The vet's partner, Dr. Young, stepped into the waiting room with a large man wearing a baseball cap.

"Hey, Abram," the man in the cap called out. "Still stuck with those troublemaking mini-mutts, I see."

"Hello, Mr. Calloway. What brings you here? A sick peacock?"

"Nope—I got myself a dog." The exotic animal rancher grinned with pride. "I've been looking for one since last summer when my peafowl and bison were attacked."

"Not by my dogs," Mr. Abram bristled. "They were—"

"—completely innocent, I know, I know. Anyhow, I came here looking for a tough bruiser to guard my livestock, and boy, did I find a dog! He went head to head with a truck, and the truck lost. Of course, the poor mutt was pretty busted up for a few months, but he's back on his feet now. Come on, Yeller."

He tugged on the leash, and a white bull terrier swaggered into the waiting room.

The eyes of the other dogs widened in horror, and no wonder, Dr. Elbright thought. Over the summer this dog had led a pack of strays who had mercilessly bullied the dogs of Silvertree. Mr. Abram's little dogs must have had at least a few run-ins with the bad-tempered bull terrier when they were strays themselves.

Yeller took one look at Pierre and lunged forward, snapping the leash out of Mr. Calloway's hand. He charged at the poodle, chasing him around the room. Mrs. Schmeck leaped onto her chair and clung to her hedgehog, which curled into a ball

17

again. Mr. Weibe's cat clawed its way up the wall and hissed at them from a hanging basket of flowers.

Mouse flew out of Mr. Abram's coat pocket and clamped his tiny teeth onto one of the bull terrier's hind legs. Old Sam latched onto the other hind leg, and Mitzy seized the dog's tail. The bull terrier lost his footing and somersaulted across the floor. A magazine rack overturned, and a lamp crashed to the floor as the barking bundle of dogs slammed into it.

"Control that brute, Mr. Calloway!" Mr. Abram cried, struggling to prevent Dare from leaping into the fray as well. "This is far too much excitement for Dare in her delicate condition."

"Cut that out, Yeller!" Mr. Calloway shouted. "Bad dog!"

The door opened, and a woman rushed in with an unconscious Yorkshire terrier in her arms. The tiny terrier's whiskers were badly singed.

Pierre darted toward the open door and turned to look at the bull terrier. To Dr. Elbright, it looked as if he were taunting the bigger dog, trying to lure it away from his companions.

"Look out, Mr. Abram!" Dr. Elbright cried. Mr. Abram was standing between the bull terrier and the door. The powerful dog knocked him sprawling onto the couch as it shot after the poodle, who whisked outside. Dare scrambled out of the old man's arms and out the door just before it swung shut. Calloway and the two vets hurried to the door, the other three dogs of Mr. Abram's pack right at their heels. Outside, Pierre was running down the icy road with the bull terrier close on his heels and Dare racing after them in spite of her heavy belly. In moments, all three were lost in the snow.

Chapter Two

Old Friends

A WEEK LATER, Pierre and Dare still had not been found.

"Where do you think you're going, young lady?" Old Sam said as Mew crept toward the pet door in Mr. Abram's house. "You're not to leave the house until Mr. Abram wakes from his nap."

"But I have to pee," she whined, doing a desperate little dance to make it more convincing.

"Oh no, you don't." Old Sam placed himself in front of the pet door. "You just want to sneak under the fence again and look for Pierre and Dare."

"No one else is looking for them!" Mew gave the basset hound a swipe with her paw, but he wouldn't move.

Mew answered to the name of Mitzy now, the name Mr. Abram had given her. He, of course, had no idea that she had been adopted and named by a farm cat when she was a puppy. The other dogs still called her Mew, though she hardly ever tried to climb trees or chase mice anymore, and she only hissed at and scratched other dogs when she was really upset.

"Mr. Abram and Calloway have been searching for them every day," Old Sam reminded her.

"Humans don't know how to search. Not once have I seen them get down on the ground to sniff a scent."

"They'll find them, don't worry."

Mew hissed with frustration. "They should have found their way home by now. Something terrible must have happened to them!"

"Someone would have told us," Old Sam assured her. "This one time, I think it's best to let the humans handle things while we stay here where it's safe."

The pet door flew open, smacking Old Sam in the rump. Two scruffy dogs poked their heads through the opening.

Old Sam nudged Mew aside. "Stand back, Mew! I'll deal with these uncivilized intruders!"

The basset hound sputtered as a three-legged, one-eyed terrier stepped into the kitchen and shook snow all over him.

Mew sneezed in surprise. "Juju!"

"And Ratter," added Ratter, the ragged white terrier who followed her in.

Juju examined her surroundings with her one good eye. "Dare was right about the wood your human used to build this house—it's from my old grain elevator. Doesn't the scent bring back memories, Ratter?"

Ratter and Dare were brother and sister, and had lived with their mother, Juju, in an old grain elevator outside of town. The family had broken up early, when Ratter had joined the Bull Dogs, a roughneck pack of stray mutts, and Dare took off to live on her own. Dare and Ratter had been enemies until Ratter left the Bull Dogs. Now the brother and sister were friendly again. Most of the time.

"I didn't know how to find your house," Juju went on, "but I found Ratter in the old badger's burrow where you Prairie Dogs used to live."

"I've never been in a human house before," Ratter said. "Nice and warm, isn't it? If I'd known I could walk in here anytime, you'd have seen a lot more of me. Hey, look! You even have your own tree, so you don't have to go outside." He trotted toward the decorated fir in the living room.

Old Sam stood in his way. "Don't even think of it!"

"Did you hear about Pierre and Dare?" Mew asked.

Juju opened her mouth and something clinked to the floor—three metal dog tags.

"I found them on the highway," she said.

Mew let out a wail of grief. "They were run over?"

"I found the *tags* on the highway. Dare and Pierre were gone. Mew, one of your cat friends—Suzie— told me they were picked up on the highway by a van heading toward the city."

"How do you know it was going to the city?" asked Mew.

"Suzie said the man who took them looked like 'a city human,'" said Ratter. He had finished Mew's breakfast, which she'd been too upset to touch. Now he was trying out their beds, wicker baskets lined with thick cushions. Mouse had never used his. He preferred to curl up in an old Frisbee with a couple of Mr. Abram's socks for a mattress. At the moment, however, he was curled up on Mr. Abram's bed. It was his turn to keep the elderly human's feet warm while he napped.

Old Sam winced as Ratter settled in his bed and began to chew the ice from between his toes.

Mew sniffed the third tag and let out a hiss. This tag belonged to the bull terrier from the pet clinic. Calloway called him "Yeller" now, but the dogs knew him as Bull, the former leader of the Bull Dogs, who had given stray dogs a bad name all over Silvertree.

"Did the human take *him* too?" Mew said.

"I'm afraid so," Juju said. "Now could someone tell me why Pierre and my daughter were on the highway in the middle of winter? And Dare in her condition! And what was Bull doing there?"

Old Sam settled his heavy haunches on the floor in preparation for a long tale. "Pierre and Dare's misadventure commenced with a routine excursion on our part to the local animal health care specialist—"

"*You* tell the story, Mew," Juju begged.

Mew began, "It all started with a trip to the vet…"

The dogs listened gravely as Mew told Juju and Ratter everything that had happened.

Chapter Three
The Dognapping

"WHAT HAPPENED to the little Yorkie?" Ratter asked, when Mew had finished her story.

"Daisy was injured in battle. She finally killed the Roaring Red Beast!" Mouse, the fainting Chihuahua, had woken from his nap with Mr. Abram and joined them just in time to catch the end of Mew's tale.

"The Roaring Red Beast was a vile creature who lived in a closet in Daisy's house. Sometimes it broke loose and sucked viciously at the floor with its wide mouth. Daisy had been helping her humans battle this monstrosity since she was a pup," Old Sam explained to the very interested Ratter.

"Daisy bit its tail," Mouse continued, his own tail wagging wildly as he recounted her courageous battle. "It had this long, black tail that had burrowed into the wall. The tail was full of lightning and it knocked Daisy right out. She's so brave!"

Mew rolled her eyes. "Could we get back to Pierre and Dare? We don't know what happened after they left the clinic."

"I do," Juju said. And she told them what Mew's cat friend Suzie had told her.

○○○○○

Suzie had been hunting for mice when she saw Pierre and Dare standing at the edge of the highway. Behind them was the town of Silvertree, and Bull. In front of them was the open prairie and the ruins of an old grain elevator.

With Bull closing in on them, they had no choice but to dash across the highway. Pierre cringed at the screech of brakes, but they made it to the other side in one piece.

Bull stopped at the edge of the highway. He whined and backed away as if the pavement were a raging river.

○○○○○

"He was afraid to cross the road, after that truck ran him down," Ratter explained.

"Let Juju finish the story," Mew said. Ratter's sympathetic tone annoyed her. As far as she was concerned, Bull deserved to get run over by a hundred trucks. Juju continued her tale, telling them everything that the cat had seen.

○○○○○

Suzie had watched as Bull took a trembling step toward the road, and another step. Meanwhile, Pierre and Dare entered the ditch, intending to cross over to the remains of Dare's birthplace. The jumble of lumber from the old grain elevator would be the perfect place for two small dogs to hide. But immediately they sank in fluffy white snow. As it closed over their heads, they realized they had made a terrible mistake.

"Dare! Are you all right?" Pierre coughed, flailing around blindly.

"Pierre, I can't move! Oh, I hate being a small dog!"

As the two dogs struggled, footsteps in the snow were coming closer, and closer...

○○○○○

"And then he got them!" Juju barked, so suddenly that Mew, Mouse, and even Old Sam jumped like rabbits. In his bedroom, Mr. Abram snorted, then resumed snoring.

"Bull?" Mouse gasped.

"No! The human that almost ran over them. He tossed Pierre and Dare into the back of his van and climbed inside. Bull ran to the van and scratched on the door. The stupid human let him inside!" Juju sneezed in disgust. "Suzie told me their collar tags flew out the window a minute later, and then the van drove away with all three dogs."

"To the city?" Old Sam asked.

"Suzie said the human who took them was a young man with wild hair and bits of metal sticking out of his face," said Ratter. "Either he'd just been in an accident, or he's a city human."

"Why would a city human take them?" Mew said.

Juju looked grim. "Suzie caught a look inside the van before the door closed, and it was full of dogs. Small, valuable purebred dogs who didn't look happy to be there. The man is a dog thief, and Pierre and Dare—and even Bull—have been stolen."

"What can we do?" Old Sam said. "We can't run all the way to the city. We can't tell Mr. Abram where Pierre and Dare are."

"Mother has a plan," Ratter said.

"You dogs will travel to the city in style," Juju said. "By train."

"Madam, you can't possibly expect us to board a

train," Old Sam said. "That's more than my old bones can tolerate. Mouse is too tiny and has no winter coat, and Mew is too young to travel so far."

"I am not!" Mew cried.

"You'd never get that heavy rump of yours onto the train, old hound, but there's no reason these youngsters can't go," Juju said. "When I lost my leg, I walked for over an hour on three legs to get back to the grain elevator. I was back on my paws as soon as the humans stitched me up. And when I lost my eye to that coyote—"

A yawn came from Mr. Abram's bedroom. The visitors hustled toward the pet door.

"When the next train rolls into town, we'll come and get you. Be ready!" Juju advised, and the two dogs left the house.

Chapter Four
Pierre's Plan

"WHAT IS THIS PLACE?" Dare asked as the van left the highway and turned onto a street lined with tall buildings. "They sure have a lot of lights."

"It's a city," Pierre said.

"Ha! I knew the metal-faced human would take us to the city," Bull said. "I should have tried hitch-hiking a long time ago. Get out of my way. Soon as that door opens, I'm out of here."

He didn't need to tell them to get out of his way. Pierre, Dare, and the other little dogs were squeezed into a corner of the van, as far from him as they could get.

A deep rumble startled the dogs. A huge jet roared over the van, so low Pierre could see the faces of the humans looking out of the little windows.

Dare flattened herself against the floor. "What's that?"

"It's a plane," he said. "Remember when we used to chase ducks off that little runway near Silvertree so the small planes could land?"

"I didn't know they grew them that big! Everything is big here. I don't like it!"

"This is my fault," Pierre said. "Didn't I say just the other day I missed the city? I jinxed us. Just like when I wished for a little freedom and adventure, and then my humans drove off and abandoned me in Silvertree."

"Wish us back with Mr. Abram, then," Dare suggested.

"And wish the dog thief into prison," said a cocker spaniel, glaring at the back of the young man's spiky-haired head.

The man parked the van in front of a building near the outskirts of the city. Before he opened the door, he slipped a chain collar around Bull's neck and clipped leashes to all of their collars. So much for escaping. A large woman with graying hair and a face like a bulldog met him at the front door of the building, which turned out to be a pet food and supply store. She and the man dragged the dogs into an untidy office in the basement. She set Pierre on a desk, ran her hands over him from nose to tail, and checked his teeth. She did the same to all the dogs.

She led the dogs out of the office and into a room full of cages. While the man wrestled Bull into one cage, the woman shoved the smaller dogs into cages already crowded. Pierre and Dare shared a cage with a pair of pugs and the tiniest apricot poodle Pierre had ever seen. Most of the dogs were quite young, some hardly more than puppies.

As the two humans went back up the stairs, the little poodle bounced to her feet and sniffed Pierre. "Are you my new mate? My name is Cupcake. I'm a teacup poodle. Maybe Beth wants me to have puppies!"

Dare growled. "Pierre is *my* mate, and I'm the one having puppies. Get your nose away from him."

"I'm very valuable," Cupcake said. "That's why I was stolen. I can't imagine why Beth made Skid steal *you*. You're just a mongrel. No one will want to buy you."

"Let's not fight," Pierre said quickly as Dare's hackles rose. "We're all in this together. Let's plan our escape. When does Beth take us out for exercise?"

"Exercise?" snorted a restless Jack Russell terrier in the cage next to theirs. "The only time we leave these cages is when she's trying to sell us."

Bull's tail gave a rare wag. "Some naïve human will buy me, and as soon as I give him the slip, I'll get myself a pack of city dogs, just like I've always wanted."

"We'll have to do the same," Pierre told Dare.

Bull laughed. "You, leading a pack of city dogs?"

"I meant wait until someone buys us, then escape."

The flaw in their plan was that no one wanted to buy them. The next day, Beth brought many wealthy-looking humans down into the basement to look at the dogs, but no one even looked at Pierre and Dare, and only one dog was sold—a Scottish terrier. The dog who attracted the most attention was a Chinese crested, pink and hairless except for wild bursts of white fur on his head, tail, and paws. Everyone looked and laughed at him, but no one bought him, either.

"It's not fair," complained a miniature dachshund, after some humans had made fun of her as well.

"They're the ones who bred us to look this way. Do they think we like being tiny and ridiculous?"

"*My* ancestors were bred small so they could go down into burrows and drive out badgers and foxes for their humans to catch," Dare pointed out. "There's nothing ridiculous about that."

"There's nothing ridiculous about any of us," said one of the pugs, a haughty expression on his small squashed face.

"After all, we are all descended from the noble wolf," added his twin.

"Noble!" Pierre snorted, remembering the half wolf who had almost killed him a few months ago. He stared at the arms pouring Crunchy Nibbles—Pierre's least favorite food in the world—into bowls. The arms belonged to Skid, the human who had dognapped them and who worked in the store with Beth. They were covered with tattoos.

"*You* have a tattoo in your ear," Dare told Pierre. "Did you know that? It's not a picture, just a row of little marks."

"Paul and Melissa, my first humans, put it there when I was a puppy," Pierre said. "My mother said it means I'm a purebred."

Dare looked at all the tattoos on the man's arms. "Then Skid must be *really* purebred."

After she closed the store, Beth pulled Pierre out of his cage and carried him to a sink in another room. She bathed him and took a pair of electric clippers to his fur, shearing off the nice thick coat Mr. Abram had let him grow for the winter. When she was finished, he had hardly any coat left at all, except for a curly ruff around his chest and silly puffs of fur on his legs, tail and head. Dare growled when Beth put him in the cage, not recognizing him. Then she howled with laughter.

"It's not funny," Pierre snapped. "I'm freezing!"

The new style made Pierre quite popular the next day. One couple even took him out of his cage so they could get a closer look at him. Dare barked and scratched on the cage door, but they ignored her. The humans weren't interested in a mongrel about to have puppies. If these people bought Pierre, Dare would be left behind.

"I can't let them buy me," he said frantically.

The other dogs barked advice.

"Bark at them!"

"Bite them!"

"Pee on their shoes!"

Pierre did none of these things. He rolled his eyes dramatically and pretended to faint.

Beth grabbed Pierre and gave him a thorough examination. Finding nothing wrong, she put him back in his cage. She tried to interest the people in the other dogs, but they shook their heads and hurried off. Beth followed them, throwing a suspicious frown over her shoulder as she climbed the stairs.

After that, Pierre threw a faint every time a human showed interest in him. The other dogs followed his example. On busy days the floor was littered with fainting dogs.

"They're just faking!" Beth cried to one woman who jingled with expensive jewelry as she rushed back up the stairs.

"That's ridiculous." The woman's voice was muffled by the collar of her fur coat, which she pressed tightly over her mouth and nose. "Where would a dog learn how to faint?"

Beth yelled at the dogs and shook her fists. They weren't worried. Beth wouldn't risk damaging her merchandise.

Bull had the opposite problem. No one wanted to buy the fierce-looking bull terrier whose coat was covered in battle scars. Bull didn't know how to act friendly toward humans. He glared at them as if they were pack members who needed to be kept in line.

"Try wagging your tail and licking their hands," Dare suggested. Bull growled in disgust.

"Dare, if someone wants to buy you, go with them," Pierre told her. "Don't worry about me. The important thing is that our puppies are born in a safe place."

Dare lay down and said, "Put your head on my stomach."

Pierre laid his head across her round belly. Something bumped against his chin, and again, like a very slow heartbeat.

"One of the pups has the hiccups," Dare said, and pressed her face against Pierre's shoulder. "I don't want to leave you. We're a family. I want us both to go back to Mr. Abram, and Mew, Mouse, and Old Sam."

"We will," Pierre said. "You and I and our hiccuppy puppies."

"Count me in," Bull said. "I want freedom more than I want revenge on you puny mutts for getting me hit by a truck. Get me out of here, poodle, and we'll call it even. I'll never lay a tooth on you again."

"Count me out!" said Sprout, the Chinese crested. "It's cold out there."

"A little cold won't hurt you," Dare said.

"Oh, really? Maybe you haven't noticed, but I have *no fur*. I'm staying here."

"What's the plan, poodle?" Bull asked.

"I'm working on it." Pierre tried to sound confident, but when he thought of all the obstacles between them and freedom, he felt sick with despair.

Sick, he thought.

"Everyone," he said, "listen closely. I have an idea."

Chapter Five

City Dogs

BETH DIDN'T COME INTO the store until noon the next day. When she walked into the basement, she let out a shriek. Skid came running. He didn't shriek, but he said some angry words.

The dogs lay on the floor of their cages, panting and drooling, their tongues lolling out of their mouths. The whites of their eyes showed beneath half-closed lids. Only the Chinese crested was still on his feet.

"They're faking," Beth said. She pulled Pierre out of his cage. He aimed a hacking cough at her face. She shoved him back into the cage, rushed to the sink, and scrubbed her face with soap.

She and Skid pulled on rubber gloves and tied

cloths around their faces. They bundled the dogs into old bedsheets and carried them out to the van. Skid jumped in and stepped on the gas. The van squealed out of the parking lot and sped down the street.

Pierre poked his head out of the sheet to check on the others.

"Stay under the sheets and don't move!" he ordered. "We have to keep absolutely still until the van stops. We'll jump out when Skid opens the door, and then we'll be free. Stop that!" he added as wagging tails made the sheets twitch.

"Where do you suppose he's taking us?" Dare said.

"To the vet, of course." Pierre was certain.

Dare wriggled free of the sheet and climbed onto a stack of boxes to look out the window. She was right behind Skid.

"Get down!" Pierre growled softly. "Do you want him to see you?"

Apparently she did, because she reached over the seat and nipped Skid's ear.

Skid gave a piercing yell. The van went into a wild spin, tires hissing and squealing across ice and pavement. The dogs were thrown around the inside of the vehicle. The boxes fell over, nearly crushing Pierre. Finally, the van bounced to a halt against the sidewalk.

Skid jumped out of the van and ran around to the back. He wrenched the door open, no doubt intending to wring Dare's neck. He found himself face to face with an angry bull terrier who didn't look sick at all.

Bull chased him several times around the van. The other dogs scrambled out of it and ran, not even looking back as Skid jumped inside, slammed the door in Bull's face, and drove away, tires squealing.

"Are you all right?" Pierre nosed Dare all over in concern. After a wild ride like that, he wouldn't have been surprised to see a pup or two pop out of her.

"I'm fine! Don't fuss so much." Dare turned away and trotted headfirst into a lamppost. She sat down and shook her head dizzily.

"That was the dumbest thing you've ever done!" Pierre exclaimed. "And that's saying a lot."

"It worked, didn't it?" Dare blinked hard as if she saw two of him. "Do you think Skid would have put us in sheets if he was taking us to the vet? He was probably going to throw us into a garbage bin, or worse!"

"You can't trust humans," Bull agreed.

"We have to trust them now," Pierre said. "We can't wander around on our own. We need some-one to take us in."

"Speak for yourself," Bull said. "I'm out of here."

"Wait!" Pierre called as Bull trotted away. "We have to stick together!"

Bull just laughed and kept going.

"He has the right idea," said one of the tiny dogs. "I never did like my humans. I'd rather be on my own."

"My humans *gave* me to Beth," said another. "I'll never trust another human again."

"My human treated me like a toy. She even dressed me up in doll clothes. From now on, I'm a rough, tough stray and nobody better mess with me!" Cupcake declared in her squeaky little bark.

And before Pierre knew it, half of Beth's dogs were gone. The rest of them huddled together, shivering and whimpering.

"Don't worry," Dare told them. "I've been on my own for most of my life, and Pierre used to be a city dog. There's nothing he doesn't know about city life. Pierre is one of the smartest dogs you'll ever meet. Right, Pierre?"

Pierre sneezed in shock. Dare had never spoken that way about him before. And it was all lies. His previous humans had kept him off the streets as much as possible. He knew no more about city life than a farm dog would.

"Right," he said, shivering in his thin coat. "The first thing we need is warm, safe shelter."

The dogs looked around. Around them loomed rundown buildings with broken windows and walls sprayed with graffiti. The sidewalks were lumpy stretches of snow and soggy trash. A human pawed through a garbage can like a stray cat looking for food. He saw the dogs and bared his few remaining teeth in a grin.

"Nice doggies," he crooned, waggling his dirty fingers at them. Then he lunged at them. They leaped out of reach and fled.

"He was going to eat us," the Maltese said.

"No, he wasn't, and not all humans are like that," Pierre assured the dogs. "Most humans are quite nice and would help us if we went up to them. Stop snorting, Dare, you're getting my fur all wet."

"How do we know they won't keep us for themselves, or try to sell us like Beth did?" she said. "Or put us in an animal shelter?"

Pierre's ears perked up. "That's it! We'll turn ourselves in to the local shelter."

The papillon's butterfly-wing ears snapped back. "No way! They'll starve and beat us and perform terrible experiments on us."

"Who told you that? They'll just give us food and warm beds until our humans come to claim us."

"How will our humans know we're there?" the dachshund asked.

"You're purebreds, right? So you all have tattoos in your ears. I'm pretty sure those markings tell the shelter humans whom you belong to."

The dogs spun around and around, trying to see inside their own ears. Pierre sighed.

The traffic noise faded for a moment, and Pierre heard dogs barking in the distance. He said, "Follow me."

He trotted into the street, and suddenly honking, skidding vehicles were all around him. As he scrambled back toward the sidewalk, a wave of crumbling snow struck him, carried him along the road a ways, and dumped him onto the sidewalk. The massive blade of a snowplow swept by.

"That was a demonstration of how not to cross the street," he said, his voice squeaking like a kitten's. "Now we'll do it the safe way."

"You mean wait until the light changes and cross with those humans on the corner?" asked the Boston terrier.

"Exactly," Pierre said, noticing for the first time a group of humans with their faces tucked into collars and hands tucked into pockets. When the streetlight changed, the dogs followed them across the street.

A few blocks of travel took them to a nicer neighborhood, with houses and trees and neat little yards. The barking of dogs grew closer until they came upon a chain-link fence around a small playground. There were no children here, only dogs. Dogs playing with balls and tug ropes and squeaky toys. Dogs climbing a blue plastic ladder and sliding down a red plastic slide. Dogs playing hide-and-seek around a little green plastic house.

"Is this the animal shelter?" Pierre asked, thinking more stray dogs would turn themselves in if they knew they'd end up in a place like this.

A sheltie bounded over to the fence. "No, this is Debbie's Doggie Daycare."

"Our humans bring us here to be cared for during the day while they're out," a boxer explained.

"Can you tell us where the animal shelter is?" Pierre asked.

"On the other side of town," a Dalmatian said. "You have nothing to worry about."

"But we *want* to go to the shelter," explained Pierre.

The Dalmatian's jaw dropped. "Are you crazy?"

A schnauzer backed away. "Maybe they have rabies."

"If it's on the other side of the city, we'll never get there," the bichon said.

The little dogs began to shiver and whimper again. Dare rolled her eyes.

"I can show you folks the way," said a border collie cross. "I was a stray once."

"Can the rest of us come along?" a schipperke said. "We could use a little adventure."

"No!" Pierre remembered the trouble he had gotten into when he left Paul and Melissa's motor home in search of "a little adventure."

But the dogs weren't listening. They pushed their

plastic slide over to the fence, climbed the ladder, and joined the small dogs on the sidewalk.

"So much for not attracting attention," Dare said.

The border collie broke into a run. "Follow me! I'll have you there quick as a lick."

"Slow down!" Pierre called. "My mate's about to have pups, you know!"

He needn't have worried about Dare. The pack traveled slowly because everyone kept stopping to sniff things. The border collie, who had a strong herding instinct, would circle back to round up the scattered pack and nip at the stragglers.

"Is it my imagination, or is our pack getting bigger?" Dare said.

Pierre looked around and gave a startled sneeze. The pack had doubled in size. Dogs were joining them from every neighborhood they passed through. They seemed to think Pierre was leading them to a great canine event.

"This is ridiculous!" Pierre cried. "We'll never get across the city with this many dogs!"

Pierre announced he was taking them all to the animal shelter, hoping it would scare them off, but they just laughed. They thought his true destination was a secret, exciting place he didn't want to share.

Dare ducked behind an Irish setter. "We just passed Beth's store! I hope she wasn't looking out the window."

45

"We've gone a long way," Pierre told the border collie. "Are you sure you know where you're going?"

"You bet! The shelter is right on the edge of town. Listen! Hear the dogs barking? We're close!"

The dogs crossed one last road and climbed a hill overlooking a large park. All across the park humans were skiing, tobogganing, or admiring enormous snow sculptures shaped like people and animals. A fat bearded man in a red suit sat on a chair of ice, laughing heartily at the humans who brought their children to sit on his knee. Everything looked soft and fuzzy behind the veil of snowflakes tumbling from the sky.

"Oops! Wrong edge." The border collie laid his ears flat against his head. "Well, shucks. We're lost."

Chapter Six

The Blizzard

"WE'RE LOST?" Pierre said.

"Yep. Sorry about that." The border collie looked sheepish. "Want me to round them up for you?"

The border collie pointed his nose at the other dogs, who had run down the hill and into the park to find the source of all the barking. Pierre was curious, too, so he, Dare, and the border collie followed them.

The barking came from a race about to get under way. Six teams of huskies, malamutes, and hardy crossbreeds strained at the traces that bound them to a row of wooden sleds. The sleds were tied to the bumpers of six trucks so the excited dogs couldn't take off before the sled drivers were ready.

"Go!" the dogs yodeled, lunging against their harnesses until the trucks rocked. "Go! Go! Go!"

The drivers of the sleds were children, and they looked as eager to start the race as their dogs.

Dare poked her nose through the orange plastic netting that held the crowds back from the dog sleds. "I didn't know dogs could pull sleds! I thought only humans and horses did that."

"It must be a new travel plan the humans have come up with." Pierre pictured a world where humans abandoned their smelly cars and went everywhere by dogsled. Instead of taking buses the humans would ride one giant sled pulled by a hundred dogs. Maybe Mr. Abram would build them a little sled so the Prairie Dogs could carry his groceries for him.

"It sure attracts a lot of attention," Dare said.

Pierre looked around. All the humans were staring at his enormous pack. "Uh-oh," he said. "I think we're the ones attracting all the attention."

The humans didn't look happy with the great number of dogs in their midst. Some of them had small phones to their ears and were speaking rapidly into them. A group of humans who had been watching over the sled dogs pushed their way through the crowd. With ropes and leashes clenched in their fists, they slowly advanced on Pierre's pack.

"Don't panic!" Pierre said to the dogs. "Hold your ground. They'll only take us to the animal shelter."

The dogs panicked, bolting in all directions. Some tried to run through the orange fence, but the plastic netting bounced them right back. Others made for the crowd, getting tangled up in legs as the humans tried to jump out of their way, stumbled, and fell. For a minute there was a confused tangle of humans and dogs rolling around in the snow. Only Beth's little dogs stood by Pierre, calmly trusting in his plan.

"Hey, Pierre," said one of the pugs, "when they check our ears at the shelter, will they call the humans who put the tattoos there? Because my brother and I don't live with those humans anymore. They sold us when we were puppies."

Pierre froze in horror. He had been thinking the shelter humans would call Mr. Abram, but it wasn't Mr. Abram who had put the tattoo in Pierre's ear. That was Paul and Melissa, his original owners, the ones who had made his life a misery. If they claimed him now and took him back to Montreal, what would happen to Dare?

"What's wrong?" Dare asked.

"Did you know some dogs have tattoos on their stomachs?" he said to Beth's dogs. While the little dogs were busy tumbling head over paws trying to look at their bellies, he whispered to Dare, "You and

49

I can't go to the shelter. Paul and Melissa will come for me!"

Now that all of the larger dogs had cleared out, the humans felt it was safe to approach the little dogs. One by one, Beth's dogs were scooped up into the arms of the humans. Pierre and Dare backed against the orange plastic fence as three humans closed in on them. There was nowhere to run.

Dare glanced over her shoulder. Six children had stepped onto the backs of the sleds. Older humans were untying them from the trucks. The dogs were so excited their barks sounded like screams.

"Come on, Pierre!" To Pierre's horror Dare slipped under the plastic netting and ran toward the sled dogs.

"No, Dare! Don't get in their way! There's no telling what they'll do!"

But Dare had no intention of getting in their way. She climbed onto the nearest sled. Pierre squirmed under the fence. A man made a grab at him, but caught only a bit of fur from his short tail. Pierre scrambled up behind Dare just as the humans untied the sled from the truck. A human who had been waving a flag dropped it suddenly to the ground.

"Hike! Hike!" the young humans shouted. The sled dogs lunged forward. Pierre and Dare were thrown against a girl sitting in the sled.

"Oops!" Dare said. They hadn't noticed the girl. She was so bundled up against the cold, she looked like part of the sled. "I hope she doesn't throw us off!"

But the girl wrapped her arms around them and held on tightly as the sled shot across the snowy field. The other girl on the back of the sled was yelling commands at the five huskies. The dogs stretched into a gallop, yelping "Go! Go! Go!" Pierre noticed they wore booties on their feet, probably to keep snow and ice from gathering between their toes.

"This is fun!" Dare stretched her nose into the icy wind. Streams of snowflakes whipped past her ears. "I think we're winning!"

The six dog teams raced across the prairie, pulling their wooden sleds up and down low hills marked by orange flags. Their young drivers yelled commands to guide them around obstacles. Coming down hills, they stepped on a brake to keep the sleds from running over the dogs.

"Haw!" the children shouted, and the sleds began to swerve to the left.

"I think we're turning around," Pierre said. "We must be going back."

"Then it's time to get off," Dare said.

"What? No, wait!"

But Dare had already squirmed out of the arms

of the girl in the sled. As the dogs slowed for the turn, Dare jumped off.

Pierre tumbled off the sled and staggered over to her. "Well, at least you didn't bite her ear and try to make the sled crash."

The five other teams thundered past them— "Go! Go! Go!"—and raced back toward the city. Pierre was pleased to see their team was still in the lead. He wasn't so pleased to be sitting in a field in the middle of nowhere. They had left the park and the city far behind.

"Well, Pierre, it's time."

Pierre turned back to Dare. "Time for what?"

"Time for the pups to arrive."

Pierre panicked. "What, now? Can't they wait?"

"Nope. And I see the perfect spot to have my puppies."

Pierre followed her gaze. In the distance, a row of grain elevators rose on the horizon.

"They're too far away. We have to find you some-place warm and safe." To his alarm, Dare trotted toward the elevators. "Where are you going?"

"I was born in an elevator. Why shouldn't my pups be?"

"It's snowing," Pierre pointed out. "We'll get lost!"

Dare ignored him. He gave up and followed her.

The dogs followed a snowmobile track that dipped and rose over the fields. When the track veered away from their destination, they slipped under a barbed wire fence and followed cattle trails through a pasture. They passed a herd of cattle huddled together in the shelter of a stand of trees. The snow stuck to their hides made them look like ghost cows.

The snow fell heavier as they left the pasture. In some places they had to lunge through shallow drifts. Pierre moved in front of Dare and pushed against the snow like a small snowplow, clearing the trail for her.

The ground beneath the snow turned slippery as Pierre stepped onto a frozen pond. He stopped and looked around. The city had disappeared. So had the elevators. He and Dare were surrounded by a swirling white wall of snow. They were lost in a blizzard in the country.

Chapter Seven

The Train Ride

IT WAS STILL dark when Mew woke and heard Ratter barking outside the fence. The dogs slipped outside. Old Sam opened the back gate with his nose.

Ratter stared at Mouse and Mew in horror. "You're wearing *that* to the city?"

"These are our traveling uniforms," Mouse said. "They're the latest fashion. We're the envy of dogs everywhere."

"Pink sweaters," Ratter said. "With pompoms and booties. Booties!"

Mrs. Buttenfield, who cleaned Mr. Abram's house once a week, had knitted fuzzy little sweaters for the dogs. Dare had already chewed hers to shreds—and buried it in the snow, to be safe.

"I don't need a sweater, but Old Sam said I had to put it on," Mew growled. He had made her and Mouse wear them since Juju and Ratter's visit, much to Mr. Abram's delight. "How touching!" he had exclaimed the first time they refused to let him take off their sweaters. "I told Mrs. Buttenfield you'd take to them eventually. I'll ask her to knit you some more."

"Keep your distance from me when we get there," Ratter said. "Pretend you don't know me."

Mouse looked at him. "You're coming with us?"

"You got a problem with that?" Ratter looked straight back at Mouse and Mew.

"No," they said doubtfully.

Juju met them near the middle of the train. It was dropping off supplies for the new concrete grain elevator the humans were building to replace the old wooden one they had knocked down. The engine throbbed like a slow heartbeat.

"You see those small holes at the back of the round cars?" Juju said. "That's where you'll stow away."

Mew stared at the long train with its many cars. Some looked like the white vitamins Mr. Abram gave the dogs to make them healthy. Some looked like the cans of dog food Mr. Abram fed them every morning. Some looked like the boxes of treats Mr. Abram gave them when he was teaching them new tricks. The man climbing into the tall red engine at the front looked exactly like Mr. Abram, except he was young instead of old, fat instead of skinny, he had no hair or mustache or glasses, and his face was brown instead of pink.

Juju misunderstood her miserable expression. "Don't be afraid, Mew. I used to ride trains all the time. It's easy. I wish I could go with you, but I can't make the jump onto the train with my missing leg. You won't make it either, old hound."

"I have no intention of being left behind," Old Sam huffed, but as he looked up at the nearest car, he realized she was right. There was no way his short legs would lift his long, heavy body onto the platform at the back of the car.

The engine's heartbeat sped up, quick as a running dog's. The train gave a thunderous series of bangs as the slack between the cars was taken up.

"Off you go!" Juju said. "Step up here, old hound, and give these youngsters a boost."

Old Sam hooked his front paws over the bottom rung of an iron ladder of a car whose sides were splashed with graffiti. Mouse climbed up the basset hound's back and bounced off his head onto the platform. Mew went next, but misjudged the distance and came crashing to the ground. Laughing, Ratter sprang easily onto the platform. Old Sam sidestepped frantically as the car began to move.

"I hate these big stupid paws!" Mew exploded. "I'm so clumsy."

"Just be grateful you have four of them," Juju said. "Try again, quick!"

This time she made it. Juju and Old Sam ran alongside their car as the train picked up speed.

"Good luck!" Juju cried. "Oh, I wish I could go with you. How I loved to ride trains when I was your age!"

"Wasn't that how you lost your leg?" Old Sam puffed as he struggled to keep up.

"Well, yes, now that you mention it." Juju looked slightly embarrassed for a moment. "Just try not to fall under the wheels like I did. Anyhow, what's a leg more or a leg less, to a dog?"

The icy wind threatened to whisk the dogs off the platform. They jumped into the opening at the back of the car, which was divided into two small caves. Ratter went in one, Mew and Mouse in the other. Dusty grains of wheat were piled in the corners. The dirty metal floor turned their pink booties black as coal. Mouse sat down, then bounced back up as if he had sat on a spring.

"The floor is like ice. We'll have to stand all the way to the city!" he complained.

"No, we won't," Ratter said from the other side. "There's a newspaper in here. Humans travel this way, too."

Mew shivered, more from excitement than cold. She had always felt jealous when Pierre told them about all the different cities he had traveled to when he was a champion agility dog. Now she was traveling herself, and by train! Pierre had never done that!

She thought of something and stuck her head back outside. Juju, barking with excitement, raced beside the train on her three little legs. Mew could barely hear her over the wind and clatter. She shouted to Juju at the top of her voice:

"Juju, how do you know this train is going to the same city as Pierre and Dare?"

Juju looked surprised. "You mean there's more than one?"

The train swept around a curve and roared across the prairie, leaving her behind.

Chapter Eight

Prairie Pups

"LET'S REST for a minute," Pierre said, trying not to sound panicky.

Dare pressed close against him. "We're lost, aren't we? It's my fault. I'm sorry."

"We're not lost. We know where we are—we just don't know where everything else is." He closed his eyes against the sharp flakes slashing at his face. He opened them just as a pale shape emerged from the blizzard.

"Help! We're lost!" he cried. "Please help us!"

The pale form paused, staring at the two dogs huddled together on the frozen pond, half buried by snow. Pierre's frantic barks trailed off as he realized it was a large white rabbit or hare, invisible except for its dark eyes and the black tips of its ears. What rabbit would help a couple of dogs? It had probably been chased by dogs all its life.

"Follow the flashing star." Its voice was a faint whisper in the howling wind.

Pierre looked up at the sky, which had already darkened with the early winter sunset. For a moment the snow cleared, and Pierre's eyes were dazzled by the flash of a bright star. When he looked down, the pale rabbit was gone. With a quiet sense of awe, he pushed forward, letting the star guide him. Dare followed. The star drew closer as they traveled, which seemed unusual behavior for a star, and it hummed to itself, a deep, mournful sound that rose and fell with the wind.

The dogs stumbled against the tallest metal tower they had ever seen. The star was a flashing light at its tip, far above the ground. The humming noise was the wind passing over the thick steel cables that anchored it to the ground. It stood next to a box-shaped building. The dogs pressed against the rough brick, taking shelter from the icy wind. Pierre saw tracks and droppings on the ground. "The rabbit was real!" he said in wonder.

Dare looked at him oddly. "What did you think it was? Of course it was real. And it saved our lives. I'll never chase one again."

"Let's get you inside. I'll try to find a way in."

"Hurry, Pierre."

Leaving Dare shivering against the wall, Pierre ran around the outside of the building. There were several doors, but no one responded to his barking and scratching. As he returned to Dare, he noticed a hole in the wall overhung by a metal hood. He sprang up and clung with his claws to the square of mesh that covered the opening. He caught a glimpse of the blades of a large fan, and then the mesh came loose and dropped into the snow with Pierre under it.

He threw off the mesh and ran back to Dare. "Dare, can you jump as high as that hole? There's a fan inside, but it's not moving."

"Jump? In my condition?" But as she drew close, they realized she wouldn't have to jump. Pierre had knocked the square of mesh against the wall, creating a helpful ramp. Dare climbed it and clawed her way into the hole. She and Pierre squeezed between the blades of the fan and trotted down a short metal duct, which creaked and rattled from their weight. At the other end was another mesh door, but it swung open when Pierre nudged it. The dogs jumped down and found themselves in a storage room big enough for a human to drive a truck into. Old desks and other junk were stacked between long rows of shelves that held wheel-shaped plastic containers.

Dare sighed with relief and curled up on an old coat someone had left on the floor.

"You won't give birth here, will you?" Pierre said.

"Why not? It's no worse than where I was born."

"It's dark, dirty, and cold. Let me look around for a better place. Can you hold on until I get back?"

"I'll tell the pups to wait, but they might not listen."

Through the open door Pierre found a room the size of a barn. On two pedestals stood a pair of giant cameras, like the small one Mr. Abram sometimes aimed at the dogs when they were playing or doing something clever. One camera pointed at one of the three empty desks and the other at a bright green wall. A few televisions with blank screens stood near the desk. Black cables thick as snakes were strewn all over the floor.

A door at the other end of the big room led to rooms that contained strange equipment with glowing lights, and more TVs than he had ever seen. In some of the rooms humans stood in front of the equipment, pushing buttons and staring intently at the TV screens. Pierre slipped quietly past the doorways until he found a room with no humans. It had a console of brightly lit buttons and a wall made up entirely of TV screens. As Pierre entered the room, thinking the warm, dark space under the console might do for Dare, he heard a toilet flush, and a door across the hall opened. Pierre pressed himself against the wall as a big bearded man in a baggy sweater slouched into the room. He sat down, stared at the TVs, and pushed a few buttons on the console. Pierre crept out of the room.

He returned to the large room with the big cameras. Maybe Dare could give birth under one of the desks. As he crossed the room, a soft glow caught his eye. It came from beneath a set of double doors he hadn't noticed before. He nudged one of the doors open. What he saw set his tail wagging.

As he rejoined Dare, he was relieved to see no pups had arrived. He touched her nose with his. "Can you walk a little way?"

"If it's not too far." She was in pain, and it made him more anxious than ever. What if something went wrong with the birthing? He longed for Mr. Abram's reassuring voice and capable hands.

He led her into the camera room and through the double doors. Dare's ears perked up. Though half the room was cold concrete and bare walls, the other half was made up to look like the living room of a house, with three armchairs and a coffee table on a soft carpet. Plastic plants against a fake wallpapered wall formed a backdrop for the scene. The soft glow Pierre had seen came from the multicolored lights strung around a live spruce tree in a corner of the room. The fresh, sharp scent of its needles filled the room.

"It's perfect." Dare rubbed her face against his. "It looks just like Mr. Abram's living room."

"The building is full of humans, but it smells like they haven't been in this room for days, so we should be safe here," said Pierre. "There's water under the tree. It tastes like sap, but it's drinkable. As for food—don't worry, I'll find something. Now let's make a bed for you on one of the chairs."

"Too high. The pups might fall off." Dare seized a cushion from the armchair and yanked it to the floor, ripping it open with her teeth.

"I don't think we should—" Pierre began, but when Dare growled at him, he shut up and helped her. Together they clawed the stuffing out of the cushion and pushed it under the tree, nudging aside a stack of gift-wrapped boxes that seemed to be empty.

"Thank you, Pierre." She licked his ear. Then she nipped him. "Now go away."

Pierre paced around the tree while Dare settled quietly down to work. At last, she called him back. She looked tired but triumphant.

"Aren't they beautiful?"

Pierre thought his new children looked like slimy gophers, but he said, "They sure are. Hello, pups. I'm your father." His tail wagged so furiously he feared it might fly off and go spinning across the room. "Where are the rest of them?"

"There are only two. Isn't that enough?"

"Two is just fine," he said quickly. "I'm relieved, actually. I've been nervous ever since Old Sam told me about a Dalmatian who gave birth to fifteen puppies."

He nosed the pups lovingly, then gasped in horror. "They're blind!" he cried. "Blind and deaf! My poor children!"

"All puppies are born blind and deaf, you dummy," Dare said. "Their eyes and ear canals don't open until they're about ten days old."

"Oh. Good." He settled down beside Dare and watched while she licked them clean. Suddenly, he felt panicky. "I can't be a father. I'm not old enough to be a father! I still feel like a puppy myself! What if I'm a terrible father? What if the puppies grow up to be like Bull because I did something wrong? What if—ouch!" Dare had bitten him to shut him up.

The soft colors of the tree lights glowed upon the new family as they curled up together and went to sleep.

Chapter Nine
Pierre Off the Air

PIERRE WAS AWAKENED by a strong urge to lift his leg. He left Dare asleep with the two puppies and returned to the vent. He jumped into a snow-drift that puffed up around him in a cloud of silver flakes. Sputtering, he struggled to the sheltered side of the building where the humans had parked a row of vans. A blue tinge to the eastern sky told him it was morning, but the stars and moon were still out. The highway that ran past the building cut a dark line through the prairie to a city overhung by hazy steam. Pierre stared at the distant skyscrapers. He and Dare could never bring the pups back to the city on their own. It was too far.

He left his mark on a tire of one of the vans and

returned to the vent. He stopped to look up at the tall metal tower that had guided them through the storm.

"I wonder why it flashes at the top," he said aloud.

"So airplanes don't crash into it at night," said a voice behind him.

Pierre jumped and looked around. A magpie stood near the building. He hadn't seen its black-and-white feathers against the snow and shadows.

"What brings a fancy little dog like yourself out to the country?" The bird hopped boldly toward him, its long tail angled upward to keep it from dragging on the ground.

Normally Pierre would have run barking at the bird. He loved chasing birds. This time he just stood and stared. No, he wasn't seeing things. The magpie held a smoldering cigarette butt in its beak. The ground around the magpie was littered with cigarette butts. Pierre wondered if the bird had smoked them all. But no, this must be a spot where the humans came out to smoke.

"It's a long story," Pierre said.

"Make it a short one," said the bird. "I hate long stories."

"My mate and I were stolen, we escaped, got lost, came here."

"Interesting. My name's Pica. That's what the humans call me."

Pierre decided to practice his fathering skills on the

bird. "You shouldn't play with those, Pica. They're not healthy."

"I don't inhale."

"You're setting a bad example for the younger birds."

"The younger birds stay away from me. They think I'm weird."

"It's turning your white feathers all yellow."

"I like yellow."

Pierre threw out the ultimate insult for a wild creature. "It makes you look like a human."

"I like humans. They throw scads of food at me when they come outside. If they forget, I drop rocks on their heads to remind them."

Pierre forgot about acting fatherly. "You have food? Could I have some, please? My mate just had puppies, and she'll wake up hungry."

The magpie flew to the top of the building and retrieved some frozen bread and bits of meat and cheese. He tossed them to the ground.

"Thanks!" Pierre took a few bites for himself and gathered the rest to carry back to Dare. He glanced up at the bird and noticed smoke drifting over the edge of the roof. "Uh, you didn't drop your cigarette on the roof, did you?"

"I did! Good thing you reminded me. I wouldn't want to start another fire."

"*Another* fire?" But the magpie had picked up his cigarette and was flying away, trailing smoke behind him like a little jet.

Dare was still asleep, so Pierre dropped his bits of food in front of her and went hunting for more. All the humans seemed to have left the building. He

searched the garbage cans in every room, but they had all been emptied. The last room he checked was the one with all the TVs on one wall. Pierre sniffed around the floor, ignoring the voices coming from the speakers above his head. The program ended and a commercial came on.

"On tomorrow's *Prairie Focus* we'll interview a man famous for his collection of exotic insects," said a woman's voice. "As well, we'll bring you the story of a Silvertree man who is searching for two courageous little canines who saved his life earlier this year."

Then a wonderfully familiar voice came out of the speakers. "Those dogs mean the world to me. I'd give anything to have them back."

Mr. Abram! Pierre leaped onto the padded chair and then onto the wide console with all the brightly lit buttons. Mr. Abram looked back at him out of the largest TV screen in the center of the wall. Pierre barked and stepped forward. His paw came down on one of the buttons, and the big screen went black. Mr. Abram's voice vanished.

Bewildered, Pierre paced back and forth across the console. Every time his paws came down on a button, the picture changed on one of the TVs, but Mr. Abram didn't come back.

Pierre had a terrible thought. Mr. Abram had died of sorrow, and his ghost was haunting Pierre.

He threw back his head and howled his grief for poor ghostly Mr. Abram.

The phone next to the console rang, making him jump. Phones were ringing all over the building. He heard running footsteps and jumped off the console. He hid beneath it just as a man charged into the room.

"What—? How did *that* happen?" He rushed over to the console. Pierre heard his hands flying over the panel, pushing buttons here and there. He picked up the ringing phone.

"CKPD-TV, Craig speaking. Hi, Joan. Yeah, I know. The signals were all messed up in the control room. There must have been a power bump from last night's blizzard. Anyhow, we're back on the air and everything looks okay. Sometimes I think the station is haunted. I could have sworn I heard howling a minute ago. Don't worry, I'll keep a close eye on things."

The man hung up and left the room. Pierre crept out from under the console and followed him into the lunchroom, where he plugged coins into a vending machine and pulled out a hotdog. He heated it in the microwave and carried it into a small room where a couch, an armchair, and a coffee table faced yet another TV, the biggest Pierre had ever seen. With a furtive look around, as if he knew someone was spying on him, he reached behind the TV and pulled out a gadget that trailed colored wires. He turned on the TV and settled into the armchair. Music, beeps, and explosions came from the TV as the man worked the controls clutched in his hands.

Pierre ignored the strange sounds. His attention was on the hotdog the man had left on the coffee table. He looked up at the human. The man muttered to himself as he pumped the small buttons with his thumbs, never taking his eyes off the TV. Pierre crept forward, snatched the hotdog off the table and ran out of the room. He didn't stop until he was back under the tree, where Dare was nursing the puppies.

"Where did the little bits of food come from?" she asked.

"This bird—well, never mind. Here's more." Pierre dropped the hotdog in front of her.

"Thank you!" Dare devoured the hotdog in a few swift bites. He told her about hearing Mr. Abram's voice and seeing his face in the TV.

Dare licked the ketchup off her muzzle and said, "When Mouse's humans left Silvertree and abandoned him, he kept imagining he saw them all over the place. That's what's happening to you. Don't worry, it will pass. You know, sooner or later a human is going to come in here and water this tree."

"I know," Pierre said. "And I have an idea about how we can hide."

Some of the empty gift-wrapped boxes under the tree were quite large. He chewed a hole in one and helped Dare carry all the bedding inside. While Dare climbed into the box with her puppies, Pierre chewed a hole in a second box for himself.

"Perfect!" Dare said. "Could you watch the puppies while I take a walk?"

Pierre lay down with the two pups to keep them warm while Dare went to the vent. They crawled all over him, poking blindly at him with their stubby noses, squeaking in disappointment when they didn't find any milk. Now that they were clean and dry he could see the male was black and the female was red. He nuzzled their soft little ears and licked their tiny heads and tried to imagine what they would be like when they grew up.

"I saw the strangest thing outside," Dare said, trotting into the room. She was covered in snow; she must have been romping around in it. "This bird—"

"A smoking magpie, I know. Dare, do you think we should be hiding like this? What if we run out of food? Maybe we should go to the human for help."

"He'd probably take us to the animal shelter, and then those awful humans you used to live with might take you away."

"But we can't hide here forever. We have to get

the pups and ourselves back to Mr. Abram. How can we do that without human help?"

"Oh, you'll think of something," Dare yawned, and went back to sleep.

Chapter Ten
The Train Crash

THE TRAIN SWAYED and rumbled down the tracks all morning. It was so noisy the dogs had to bark at the top of their lungs to make themselves heard. Now and then they stuck their heads out of the metal cave to watch the prairie roll by, although they couldn't see much. It seemed to take forever for the sun to rise.

"I hate this time of year," Ratter said. "The days get so short."

"I hope they turn it around soon," Mew said.

"Who's 'they'?"

"The humans. I wonder why they decided to shorten the days in the first place."

Ratter rolled his eyes. "This is what comes of

75

spending too much time around humans. It's time you Prairie Dogs went back to being on your own."

Mouse shuddered. "Never! I remember last winter. I spent all my time trying not to freeze to death, and there was never enough to eat. The only good thing was there weren't many scents for Dare to collect."

Mew remembered all the summer nights Dare had returned to the burrow proudly reeking of some dead thing she had rolled on. Thanks to Mr. Abram and a good supply of soap, those smelly days were behind them.

The memory of smelly days made Mew think of Pitterpaw, Moonstripe, and Squirt, the skunks who had moved into the burrow with Ratter. They were hibernating now. She felt sorry for Ratter, spending the long winter nights under the ground with no one to talk to.

"That human of yours has spoiled you rotten!" Ratter scoffed. "Warm house, soft beds, rich food— and all those toys he bought you! I sniffed out even more toys in those boxes under your tree."

"Really?" Mew's tail thumped the floor. "Was there a new squeaky ball? Or a tug rope? Or a stuffed mouse? Or a—"

"We don't stay with Mr. Abram because of toys and warm beds," Mouse interrupted. "We stay because he loves us, and we love him."

"Oh, come on." Ratter looked hard at Mouse.

"Don't you miss being a stray? The freedom, the fun, the fighting? That's how animals are meant to live. Hey, after we find my sister and Pierre, why don't you give up the soft life and start a new pack with me?"

Mew wondered if that was the real reason Ratter had come along—to start a new pack in the city, like Bull had wanted to do.

"Why don't you get back together with the Bull Dogs?" Mouse asked.

"Without Bull to lead them, they all went home or to the shelter."

"What you need is a human of your own," Mew said.

Ratter made a coughing sound of disgust. "I don't know what you see in those humans."

"If you'd seen Mr. Abram trying to find Pierre and Dare, you would understand," Mouse said. He hopped out of the cave and stood boldly on the platform, although the icy wind made him shiver so hard he looked blurry.

"Look! There it is!"

Mew joined him on the platform. Her heart lifted at the sight of skyscrapers in the distance.

"Look at all the buildings! They're so *tall*," she said.

Ratter shuddered. "I can't even imagine how many humans must be in them."

Mew remembered how impressed she had been with the number of humans in Silvertree after she left the farm. Silvertree was a speck compared to this place!

The train stopped at a rail yard beside a row of grain elevators. The dogs crouched low in their metal cave as humans tramped past the train. Mew risked a peek outside and saw a human blowing hot air on a switch with a sort of vacuum-cleaner tool to clear the track of snow and ice. Finally, the train started off again. It passed a brick building with a tall metal tower and thundered toward the city.

"What if it doesn't stop in the city?" Mew asked.

"We'll have to jump off," Mouse said, and aimed a worried glance at his paws. Mew knew he was thinking of Juju and her missing leg.

"It will stop," Ratter said. "Listen—three short whistles. That means the train will stop at the next station."

The train slowed as it entered the city. The dogs stared at the traffic and the crowds of humans trudging along the snowy sidewalks. It was all very exciting, but Mew felt no wish to be a city dog. It was noisy and smelly, for one thing. There were hardly any animals, just a few sparrows and pigeons and the occasional dog or cat.

The train whistled again, two long, one short, and one long.

"That means we're approaching a road crossing," Ratter said.

The train let off a series of short whistles.

"Uh-oh," Ratter said.

"What does that mean?" Mew asked.

The train gave a whistle that went on and on without stopping.

"It means we'd better brace ourselves."

There was a squeal as the wheels locked, and the dogs were thrown into a tangled heap against the wall of their metal cave. The squealing went on and on, until there was a tremendous crash.

Mew struggled to her feet. "What happened?"

Ratter went onto the platform and looked toward the front of the train. "The train hit a car that got stuck in the snow crossing the tracks."

"Oh no! Let's see if anyone's hurt."

They jumped down and ran to the front of the train. A car lay crumpled against the tall engine. Humans surrounded it, fighting to get one of the doors open. The dogs watched as police cars, an ambulance, a fire truck, and vans with camera-carrying humans arrived.

Mew's heart was beating hard. All the shouting people and wailing sirens terrified her, but she thought she was doing a good job of hiding it.

"Cut that out!" Ratter said. "You're attracting attention."

Mew realized she was arching her back and puffing out her fur and tail. No wonder her sweater felt tight. She made herself stop, but humans were still staring at the dogs. She nudged the other two toward a big man wearing a cowboy hat so everyone would think they belonged with him. When Mouse bumped into his cowboy boots, the man looked down and jumped back in horror. When they moved toward him, he shooed them away. Mew supposed he didn't want the other humans to think he was the sort of man who would knit fuzzy pink sweaters for little dogs.

Finally, the humans got the door open and put the man on a stretcher, which they lifted into the ambulance. He was yelling at the driver of the train. Maybe he thought the train should have tried to swerve around him.

"He doesn't look too badly hurt," Ratter said. "Let's go."

Mew looked around her and shivered in despair. The city was so much bigger than any of them had imagined, and the sidewalks were thick with fresh snow. How were they supposed to find Pierre and Dare? It would take days and days to search the city.

"Mew!" Mouse gasped. "Pierre's scent is on this tire!"

He stood beside the van used by one of the camera humans. Mew came over and analyzed the scent with her sensitive beagle nose. "You're right! It's fresh, too. Do you suppose this is the van that took them away from Silvertree?"

"There's no way to tell without getting inside."

"When the humans come back and open the doors, distract them. I'll jump in and grab a quick sniff before they toss me out."

Two men returned to the van and put a camera and some other equipment into the back. Mouse tugged at their pant legs to catch their attention, but they didn't even notice. Their eyes were on a pretty young woman putting a camera into another van. They went over to talk to her, leaving the doors open.

Mew jumped into the van.

"Is his scent in there?" Mouse asked.

"No."

"It must have been parked somewhere and Pierre just happened to be passing by when he marked it. At least we know he's in the city. Come on, let's go."

"No," Mew said. "This van is our only connection to Pierre and Dare. When it leaves, we're going with it. Get up here."

"What?" Mouse squealed. "I can't even jump that high!"

"Sure you can," Ratter said, and nipped his tail. Mouse yelped and leaped into the van. Ratter followed. The van had no back seat, so they squeezed under the front seats. The humans finished their conversation and came back to the van. They slammed the rear doors, got in the front, and drove away.

A crackly voice emerged from a radio at the front of the van, and one of the humans answered it. The van sped up for a few minutes, then stopped. The two humans jumped out, pulled their equipment out of the back, and slammed the doors.

The roof of the van flickered with an orange glow. Mew jumped onto the driver's seat and looked out the window.

"A fire!" she exclaimed.

A small house had caught fire. Mew had seen farmers burning crop stubble in their fields, but she had never seen a house fire before. It was terrifying. The fire seemed like a living thing trying to devour the poor little house.

Mouse, panicking, barked at the fire.

"Good thinking," Ratter said. "That'll put it out."

Fire trucks had already arrived. Their hoses poured water through the windows and door. Thick clouds of steam rolled into the cold blue sky. The two humans had their camera pointed at the house, which was already covered in thick icicles. After the fire went out, the camera humans spoke to several people who were standing nearby. Then they brought their equipment back to the van and drove away from the fire.

The radio spoke again, and again the van sped up.

When it stopped and the humans had taken their camera out again, the dogs looked outside to see that police cars had surrounded a gas station. Several police officers came out of the building, leading an angry man with his arms bound behind his back.

"This is fun!" Mew said. "These humans know where all the exciting stuff is happening."

The van rushed to one more event, a car that had crashed into a bridge railing. It had almost fallen into the icy water. The humans drove and parked the van one more time, unloaded the equipment, and slammed the doors. The dogs looked out the window, expecting to see another exciting event, but all they saw was a parking lot behind a brick building out in the country. The sky had just gone dark, so it must be suppertime.

"We have to get out of here," Ratter said. "Next time they open the doors, make a break for it. Who cares if they see us? We can outrun them."

They crouched by the doors, waiting for the humans to come back. As time passed and the darkness deepened, the dogs realized the humans weren't coming back. They were locked in the van for the night, and the temperature was falling.

Chapter Eleven
Hunter and Hunted

WHILE DARE and the puppies slept, Pierre spied on the humans.

As the sun appeared, so did the humans who worked in the TV building. They rushed around clutching papers, cameras, and other equipment and speaking to one another in brisk voices. Just before lunchtime, their activity increased to a frantic pace. Pierre was exploring the camera barn when the room suddenly blazed with light from the heavy lights that hung from the high ceiling. A man and woman entered the room. Pierre hid under a wide desk. To his horror, the humans hurried straight over to it and sat down. Pierre backed into a corner, trying to avoid their feet. For the next half hour they sat without moving and talked to two humans standing behind the two large cameras. Pierre put his eye to the small space between the bottom of the desk and the floor. He saw Dare poke her head through the double doors of the tree room, no doubt wondering where Pierre was. She withdrew as another man rushed into the camera barn. The man stood in front of a green wall, speaking to one of the cameras and pointing at the wall as if there was a picture on it. "Forecast" seemed to be his favorite word.

Finally, everyone finished the bizarre conversation and left. Pierre escaped to the tree room, the one place in the building no one seemed interested in. At suppertime, the camera barn lights came on again, and again the humans sat behind the desk to talk to the cameras. Pierre and Dare watched them from the doorway of the tree room. After a while, they decided their puppies were more interesting than this, and went back under the tree to cuddle them.

Dare thought they needed another cleaning. They each took a puppy and washed it from nose to tail. Pierre realized when he was done that he had licked the puppy the wrong way, so all his downy black fur stood on end.

"He looks like Skid," Dare said.

The next time they ventured out of the tree

room, the humans had left the building. Only the bearded man who had been there the night before remained. He was dozing in his chair.

Pierre went outside. Pica was gone, but he had left a few bits of food on the ground. Pierre brought them back to Dare, along with a few scraps of left-over lunches in the lunchroom garbage can.

"Save some for yourself," Dare said.

"I ate already," he lied. He had already emptied the garbage can. He searched the rest of the building for food. Finding nothing, he returned to Dare and the puppies and fell into a restless, hungry sleep.

When he woke in the morning, it occurred to him that the bearded man might have eaten during the night and thrown leftovers in the garbage can. He raced toward the lunchroom. As he ran across the lobby, the bearded man stepped out of the lunchroom directly in front of him. He was in the middle of a wide yawn. Pierre skidded between the man's legs and slid to a stop behind him as the man finished his yawn and opened his eyes. The man aimed a puzzled glance at his shoes, checked to make sure his laces were tied, then shrugged and went into the room with the noisy game. He put a sandwich on the coffee table, sat down, and picked up the game controls.

Pierre knew attempting another theft was pushing his luck, but he crept into the room and up to

the coffee table. He eased his front paws onto the table and was just about to take the sandwich in his teeth when the lights went out.

The man bellowed an angry word as the TV screen went black. He jumped up and lunged toward the door, but in the dark room he ran straight into the coffee table. As he threw his arms forward to catch his balance, his hand came down on Pierre's curly head.

The man screamed and crashed to the floor. Pierre scrambled out from under him—more screaming!—and shot out of the room just as the lights came back on. Machines in every room beeped and howled, and many of the TV screens had gone dark.

"I think one of the humans is going to search the building," he panted as he burst into the tree room.

"Why do you think that?"

"It's just a feeling I have," he said mysteriously.

They climbed into their boxes just as the lights came on. The man stood in the doorway with a small phone to his ear.

"...fox, maybe. No—no, it was bigger than a fox. Maybe a coyote got in here—or a wolf! Wasn't there a vicious wolf got shot around Silvertree earlier this year?" The footsteps came closer. "Something's been in here, all right. One of the chairs on the *Prairie Focus* set has been torn up."

The man explored the space behind the fake wall of the fake living room, then left the room, and just in time, because the puppies began to cry. Dare nursed them, but when they had finished they cried again.

"What's wrong with them?" Pierre asked anxiously.

"I don't think I'm making enough milk for them," Dare said. "I'm so hungry!"

"There's just not enough food around here. Will you and the puppies be all right if I go outside to look for food? I might be gone a while."

"We'll be fine. Be careful out there."

Pierre nuzzled her ear and gave each of his children a lick on the head, then returned to the vent. He fell into a wet snowbank and scrambled out before it could soak his fur. The sun was just coming up over the horizon and all the snow had turned sparkling gold. He heard a buzzing noise and looked around curiously—bees in the winter? No, it was a lone human on a snowmobile, bouncing over the snowdrifts in the distance.

As Pierre trotted into the fields, a gravelly voice called, "What about the other dogs?"

The magpie, Pica, was hopping around the parking lot. He picked up a smoldering cigarette butt.

"Dare and the puppies will be fine."

"I meant the dogs in the van."

Pierre looked at the vans in the parking lot. "I don't see any dogs."

"They're lying on the seat. They've been in there all night."

"That's ridiculous. Why would the humans leave dogs in a van all night?"

"I'm sure they had a good reason."

Pierre snorted. "Well, I don't have time to worry about your van dogs. I have to find food for my mate."

"Sometimes I find food on farms."

Pierre's ears perked up. "Dare and I passed a farm on the way here. Thanks, Pica!"

Pierre trotted along the fresh snowmobile tracks that crisscrossed the fields between the TV building and the city. A Chinook wind had warmed the winter air, which seemed a blessing at first for Pierre and his thin coat. The sun inched higher, catching his shadow and stretching it across the snow. At the top of a hill Pierre sprang up and down a few times just to watch his shadow leap away to the next hill and back. On his last bounce his paws broke through the melting crust of snow, soaking his legs and stomach.

By the time he reached the cow pasture he and Dare had crossed two nights ago, he was shivering, tired, and hungry, but he ducked under the barbed wire fence and kept going.

The cows had visitors. They looked like deer but smaller, with only two little curved prongs on their thick black antlers. They were pulling hay from a large round bale near the cows, who didn't seem to mind.

"They're pronghorn antelope." Pica landed on a fence post. "They look harmless, but don't go near them, or you'll get a prong up your tail feathers. Aren't you going to wait for the other dogs?"

"You mean the van dogs?"

"They left the van. Now they're following your trail."

Pierre looked around, but he was surrounded by

low hills and could see nothing but snow, sky, cows, and antelope.

"What do these dogs look like?"

"Like dogs. Ears, paws, waggy tails. They're pink and white."

The only pink and white dog he had ever met was Sprout, the Chinese crested, and he could hardly imagine a pack of hairless little dogs pursuing him across the winter prairie. All that smoking must have ruined the poor bird's brain.

"Thank you for telling me about the pink dogs," he said kindly, and went on his way.

"Watch out for the farm dog," Pica called. "It has a blue tongue."

"Right." Pierre rolled his eyes.

He crossed the pasture, barking a friendly greeting at the cows. They jumped and trotted away, darting wary looks over their shoulders.

Suddenly, the antelope bounded away, their white rump patches fanning out a bright warning of danger. He thought his bark had frightened them, but then he heard a deeper, angrier bark. A big, mean-looking Chow cross guarded the farmyard. He had seen Pierre in the pasture and was tearing after him, teeth bared, and he did indeed have a blue tongue. Pierre cleared out of the pasture and took refuge in a patch of wild rose thornbushes. The Chow cross circled the bushes, barking threats and insults. Then he charged off in the direction the antelope had gone.

"As if he'll ever catch them." The thorns crackled as Pica settled heavily on one of the branches. "It's just as well. If he keeps running, he won't see the other dogs."

"The pink ones? Are they still following me?" Pierre came out of the bushes, careful not to catch his long, curly ears on the thorns. Last summer he had become ear-entangled in a thornbush, and it had taken the other dogs forever to free him. They still teased him about it.

"They're here now," Pica said.

Pierre decided to humor the addled bird. He said to the invisible dogs, "I'm pleased to meet you. Nice weather we're having, isn't it?"

Pierre heard barking, and running paws on the snow. He whirled around. A low rise stood between him and the approaching dogs. The dogs crested the small hill, panting, barking his name, the one in the lead tripping over her paws and tumbling down the hill—"

"Pierre!" Mew cried as she crashed into him. "Mouse, Ratter, we found him!"

Chapter Twelve

The Crunchy Nibbles Bandits

"HOW DID YOU GET HERE?" Pierre said, dizzy with astonishment and with the effort of keeping track of them as they ran joyful circles around him. The pompoms on their pink sweaters bounced wildly around their ears.

"By train," Mouse said casually, as if he rode them all the time.

Mew was yipping nonstop with excitement. "It was Juju's idea. But our train crashed, and then we got into the camera van and drove all over the place; there was a fire and all kinds of wild stuff going on. And we just saw an owl! It swooped right

93

over us. It was all white with feathers on its feet! I think it was going after Mouse, but it got scared off by his sweater. He went and fainted—Mouse, I mean, not the owl. That's why it took us so long to catch up to you."

"Speaking of birds," Ratter said, eyeing Pica, "am I imagining things, or is that magpie smoking a cigarette?"

Pierre started to explain, but Mouse cut him off to ask about Dare.

"She's inside the building with the tall tower. She had her puppies there," Pierre said, which set off another round of happy frisking and yipping.

"I'm an uncle!" Ratter exclaimed. "But what about Bull?"

Pierre told them about Skid and Beth and the escape from the pet store. They described Juju's plan to get them to the city, and their adventure in the van.

"You're lucky you didn't freeze to death in there," Pierre said.

"I'm used to the cold," Ratter said. "I do live in a burrow, you know. And these two had their silly sweaters."

"Some humans opened the door and we got away while their backs were turned," Mouse explained.

"I'll bet they're on their way to another fire or

something," Mew said. "Those camera humans know where all the exciting stuff is going on. But Pierre, what are you doing way out here if Dare's in the TV building?"

"We've run out of food. I was going to search that farm for food, but the farm dog won't let me near it."

"Let's look for food in the city!" Mew said. "We'll help."

"I'll help, too," Pica said. "I'll fly over the city and come back to tell you where the food is. But first I'll take care of that farm dog."

Pica spread his glossy black-and-white wings and flew across the pasture, swooping up and down as he swept the cold air currents with his long tail. The farm dog had just returned. Pica dropped his cigarette on the dog's head, pulled at its tail with his

beak, and flapped away, laughing. The dog tore after him, barking madly.

"I like that bird," Ratter said.

"Mouse, will you go back to the TV building and stay with Dare and the puppies?" Pierre asked. "I don't like leaving them alone. You can get in through a vent at the back."

Mouse stood as tall as a Chihuahua could stand. "You can count on me, Pierre. I'll look after them."

As Mouse scampered away across the prairie, Pierre, Mew, and Ratter began the long journey to the city.

"What's this?" Mew stopped to sniff at the snow. "It smells like a lot of big dogs were running around here."

"Those were the sled dogs that took Dare and me away from the city."

"You see?" Mew said to Ratter when Pierre described the sleds and the rugged dogs who pulled them. "All the cool dogs wear booties."

Pica sailed past them as they crossed the park on the outskirts of the city.

"I didn't find food, but I found a dog who knows how to get food," the magpie said. He flew over to a snow sculpture shaped like a doghouse. It even had a floppy-eared snowdog lying on its back on the roof. Pica perched on the dog's round nose and said, "Here he is."

A white dog came out of the doghouse and shook the frost out of his fur.

"Bull!" Ratter exclaimed.

"Hey, Ratter! How did you and cat brat get here?"

Mew's fur stood on end. She charged at Bull, hissing.

"It's your fault Pierre and Dare and their puppies got stuck in the city!" For a little dog in a pink sweater, she looked very fierce. "I'm going to bite your tail off!"

Pierre jumped in her way. "You're a Prairie Dog, Mew, not a Bull Dog. We don't go around attacking other dogs."

"Can't I just scratch him a little?"

"Oh no, you don't!" A pack of small dogs charged out of the icy doghouse.

"You stay away from our leader!" a Pomeranian yipped.

Mew cocked her head in astonishment. "Your what?"

"Our pack leader," said a Pekinese. The little dogs leaped and pawed affectionately at the bull terrier.

"Get down!" Bull roared. "Have some dignity, for crying out loud! You're Bull Dogs!"

The missing dogs from Beth's store had changed in the last two days. No shivering and whimpering for them. They walked with a swagger, and there was a hard glint in their little eyes.

"Next thing you know they'll be challenging him for pack leader," Ratter said to Pierre.

"I never realized it before, but there are advantages to having a pack of small dogs," Bull said. "They're easy to feed. They're too little to attract attention, which is good for stealing stuff and spying on enemy packs. And smart! We won't fight our rivals, we'll just outsmart 'em."

"You better believe it!" Cupcake piped up.

"That's the tiniest poodle I've ever seen," Ratter said. "She's even smaller than the Chihuahua."

"Don't get any ideas! Pierre is my mate," the teacup poodle said as she frisked playfully all over him. "He came back just for me."

Ratter bristled at Pierre. "Are you cheating on my sister?"

"I didn't come back for Cupcake," said Pierre hastily. "I came back for food. Bull, Dare is running out of milk for our new pups. Can you help us find some? Food, I mean, not milk."

Bull laughed. "Can I find you some food? Boy, can I ever! How would you like to raid a dog food plant?"

"A dog food plant?" Pierre pictured a bush with nuggets of dog food hanging like berries from its branches.

"Come on, I'll show you."

Bull and his little Bull Dogs took them to a

building twice the size of the TV building. The parking lot held a row of large trucks and one van. Pierre stretched his nose toward the building and inhaled the pungent aroma of—

"Crunchy Nibbles!" he cried in dismay.

"Don't be fussy, poodle," Bull scowled. "Do you want to feed that mate of yours or not? My pack and I tried to break into the place last night, but we set off an alarm. Go ahead, think up one of your heroic stunts to get us inside. I'll bet you know how to turn alarms off. Or maybe you can get into one of those trucks full of dog food and drive it away. Or—"

"Why don't you just push the button?" Pica landed on the edge of the roof.

"What button, Pica?" Pierre asked.

"The big round one."

The dogs saw a large metal disc on the wall beside the front door. Mew took a running leap at it. She meant to hit it with her paws, but tripped and hit it with her head. She shook her throbbing skull and made an angry spitting noise.

"Stupid clumsy paws! I can't do anything right."

Pierre gave her head a comforting lick. "You've done everything right! You and Mouse came all this way to help Dare and me. Clumsy paws don't matter, Mew. Not when they're attached to a dog with a brave heart."

That put the wag back in her tail. "Oh, look!" she cried. "The doors!"

The outer and inner doors were swinging open.

"You mean it's that easy to get into a building?" Bull cried. "This changes everything!"

The Bull Dogs slipped inside. Mew bounded after them.

"You'll make a fine daddy, little dog," Pica said.

"Thanks, Pica."

The doors were swinging shut again, so Pierre scooted inside. The dogs had stopped in front of the reception desk in the lobby. They heard someone behind the desk—a woman, judging by the perfume—lean forward to see why the doors had opened. They pressed against the desk, holding their breath. When the doors swung shut she sat back down and resumed tapping at something on her desk. The clicking of her fingernails masked the clicking of the dogs' claws as they edged around the desk and into a hallway. Their noses led them to a room with even more complicated equipment than Pierre had seen at the TV building. The dogs stared curiously at all the gears, rollers, chutes, and hoses. Mew ran up and down the long conveyor belts, pretending she was a Crunchy Nibble.

"Someone's coming!" Ratter warned.

Mew jumped off the conveyor belt, slid down a chute, and tumbled into one of the bins full of different flavors of Crunchy Nibbles. Pierre jumped in after her. He heard the other dogs scramble for hiding places, and then he heard crunching noises.

"Whoever's eating, stop it!" Bull commanded. The crunching noises stopped.

Pierre peeked over the edge of the bin. Several men came into the room. They pushed buttons and flipped levers, and all the equipment rumbled to life. The conveyor belts moved the food through all the equipment, poured it into bags, and sealed the bags tightly. The men watched carefully to make sure everything was working correctly. One by one, the dogs slipped out of their hiding places and crept out of the room.

Down the hall they found an even larger room. The dogs looked around in awe. Thousands of boxes and bags of Crunchy Nibbles were stacked on wooden pallets, waiting to be loaded onto the big trucks.

"I had no idea the humans worked so hard to feed us," Pierre said with a lump in his throat. "They built this huge building and all that equipment just to make our food!"

"Humans really love dogs, don't they?" the Pomeranian said wistfully.

One of the other dogs began to whimper. "I miss my human. I want to go home."

"Me, too," another said. "They weren't that bad."

Suddenly, all of Bull's little dogs were crying.

"Now look what you've done!" Bull snapped at Pierre.

Pierre heard a squeaking noise and ordered the dogs to hide behind the pallets. A man with wild hair and bits of metal in his face came into the room pushing a wheeled thing with a wooden pallet on it. The pallet was stacked with bags of dog food.

Pierre sneezed in surprise. "It's Skid! What's he doing here?"

"He must work here, too," Bull said.

Curious, the dogs quietly followed Skid. He wheeled the dog food through the large room and out the back door. After a quick, furtive look around, he opened the back door of the van and threw the bags of Crunchy Nibbles inside.

"He's stealing," Bull said. "I know a thief when I see one. I'll bet he takes the stuff back to the store so Beth can sell it."

"Stealing dog food!" Mew said. "How low can you get!"

"Isn't that what we're doing?" Cupcake said.

"Oh yeah."

"This is great!" Pierre's tail wagged furiously, trying to keep up with his thoughts. "He's doing all our work for us. Beth's store is close to the park. We can just ride along in the van, and when he stops at the store, Bull can chase him away while the rest of us take off with the smaller bags."

"This is one smart poodle!" Bull said. "Are you sure you don't want to join my pack?"

"Once was enough. I just want to stay a Prairie Dog."

When Skid went back inside for another load, Pierre, Mew, Ratter, Cupcake, and Bull hid in the van behind the stacks of bags.

"Get up here, you guys," Bull said to his pack. But they turned around and trotted back into the building.

"We've decided to go back to living with humans," the Pomeranian said over his shoulder. "But first, we're going to spend a night in the Crunchy Nibbles plant!"

Pierre imagined the dog food workers coming in the next morning to find their building full of round-bellied little dogs too stuffed to move.

Bull growled. "That's the second pack you've ruined for me, poodle. I'm starting to reconsider my promise never to lay a tooth on you again."

Skid came back with one last load of bags. Pierre wondered if he would smell the dogs when he got into the van. He did wrinkle his nose and sniff at his armpits, but then started the van and got it moving.

"Get ready to chase him away," Pierre said to Bull as the van pulled to a stop. Skid sat there with the motor running. Pierre risked a quick look out the window to make sure they were at Beth's store.

"What's he waiting for?" Bull said.

"I don't know," Pierre said. "He's just sitting there."

"Well, if he's not going to get out on his own, I'll make him get out," Bull growled, rising up from the bags of Crunchy Nibbles.

"No, wait!" Pierre cried. But Bull had already leaped into the front seat and nipped Skid's ear.

Skid screamed. His foot, which had been resting on the brake, kicked the gas pedal. The van shot forward, squealed across the parking lot, and smashed right through the plate glass of the store's front window.

Chapter Thirteen

Heroic Stunts

PIERRE DRAGGED HIMSELF to his feet and looked around in a daze. The van had stalled half in and half out of the store window. The floor was a sea of Crunchy Nibbles from broken bags. The dogs were scattered around the inside of the van in various undignified positions.

The back door opened and Pierre tumbled out in an avalanche of Crunchy Nibbles.

"You!" A meaty hand picked him up by the scruff of the neck. Beth's bulldog face loomed before him. "I knew you were trouble the moment Skid brought you in here! I'm going to wring your curly little neck! *Ouch!*"

Mew had reached out of the back of the van and

bitten Beth on the rump, startling the woman so badly she dropped Pierre.

"Run!" Pierre barked, his paws already running as they hit the ground.

Beth made a grab for the dogs, but she was too slow. Mew shot out of the van with Ratter, Cupcake, and Bull right behind her.

"This has been one disgraceful episode," Bull said when they were well away from the store. "I'm embarrassed I ever asked you to join my pack, poodle."

Pierre felt terrible. They had escaped, but they wouldn't be able to bring food back for Dare and the puppies.

Pica sailed out of the sky and landed on the hood of a car. "My goodness, you little dogs are hard to keep up with. I wish you'd stay in one spot!"

A police car and a fire truck roared by. Mew gave an excited yip and chased after them.

"Mew, come back here!" Pierre and the other dogs raced after her, all the way back to the store.

The van was still stuck halfway through the window, and it had attracted a good deal of attention. A crowd had gathered, and firefighters were examining the van and the window. Two police officers were talking to Beth and Skid, who looked very nervous.

"A van crashing into a store is *exciting*," Mew said when Pierre scolded her for running off. "And you know what that means!"

"You go ahead and watch the excitement," Bull said. "I just want out of here. What about you, Ratter? You want to start a new pack with me?"

Ratter's ears perked up, then twitched thoughtfully. At last he said, "No, I think I'll stick with these guys. Being a stray is a lonely, hungry life, even if you're with a pack. A dog is much better off with humans. What's *your* problem?" Ratter said to Pierre and Mew, who were sneezing in astonishment. "All right, I admit it, I want a human of my own. But a top quality human, like your Mr. Abram."

Pierre had a terrible thought. Ratter would come back to Silvertree with them, and kind old Mr. Abram would adopt him.

"I'd like to meet this Mr. Abram," said Cupcake, which gave Pierre another terrible thought.

A van pulled into the parking lot, and Mew did a happy little dance.

"There it is! The camera van! I knew it would come. We don't have to walk back to the TV building. We can catch a ride!"

"The parking lot is full of humans," Ratter pointed out. "How will we get past them?"

"We need someone to distract them," Pierre said.

Everyone looked at Bull.

"I can't believe I'm doing you all these favors," Bull growled. "What would my old pack think if they knew I was catering to the pussyfoot poodle who nearly got me killed?"

Bull swaggered into the middle of the parking lot. All the humans stopped to look at him, and the man holding the camera turned it toward the bull terrier.

"Hey, Pierre," Bull said over his shoulder. "If you ever get back to Silvertree, make sure you jump on a train and come back to the city once in a while. I hate to admit it, but life will be kind of dull without you Prairie Dogs." He turned to look at one of the police officers. His eyes narrowed. "I never did like cops."

He bolted across the parking lot and launched his powerful frame at the startled man. The two of them hit the ground and there was a brief struggle. Suddenly, Bull was running away with the officer's gun held firmly in his mouth.

This was a lot more exciting than a van stuck in a store window. The humans stampeded after the gun thief, leaving the parking lot nearly empty.

Pierre ran toward the camera van, then stopped. "I can't go back to the TV building without food for Dare."

The dogs looked at Beth's store, thinking of all those bags of food lying on the shelves. Beth and Skid stood outside the broken window, but they were busy talking to the firefighters.

The dogs crept over to the window. Keeping Skid's van between them and the humans, they managed to get into the store without being seen. The store was a mess. Pierre almost felt sorry for Beth and Skid.

"Who's that barking?" Mew asked.

"That's Sprout. Beth must not have sold him yet." The Chinese crested's lonely, frightened barks saddened Pierre. "I wish we could set him free."

"Is he in a cage? I know how to open cage doors," Ratter said. "That was my job when I was a Bull Dog. Springing pack members that got caught."

Pierre dropped the bag of food he had pulled off a shelf. "Let's do it!"

"You're back!" said Sprout as the dogs bounded down the stairs. "Couldn't handle life on the streets?"

"Life on the streets is better than life in a cage." Ratter flipped the latch with his nose. The door sprang open and Sprout hopped out. The dogs bounded back up the stairs.

"Everyone grab a bag of food and head for the van!" Pierre ordered.

He should have given clearer instructions. Sprout grabbed a package of birdseed and ran toward Skid's van. The dogs raced toward him, trying to head him off, and suddenly crashed into two pairs of human legs that stepped through the window.

Hands swooped down, lifting the dogs off the floor.

"Oh no, you don't." Beth squashed Pierre and Mew under her heavy arms. Skid had a tight grip on Ratter, Sprout, and Cupcake. "There's no escape for you this time, you little troublemakers!"

She gave a shriek as a large camera with a human behind it came through the window. Another human thrust a cone-shaped object into Beth's face.

"Are these dogs injured?" he asked while his partner pointed the camera at Beth and Skid. "I hope you're not selling them. They don't look very well cared for."

"The dogs are fine!" Beth said quickly. "They just need a bath, that's all. I don't sell dogs. These are my own dogs. I've had them for years. We're very fond of each other. Ouch!" Mew had nipped her arm.

As soon as the camera humans left, Beth and Skid rushed the dogs into the basement and shoved them into the cages.

"If those reporters show these dogs on the news, someone might recognize them," Beth hissed. "We've got to get them out of here before their owners show up."

"Should we set them loose?" Skid asked.

"Not if they keep finding their way back here." Beth glared at Pierre. "As soon as things settle down here, we're getting rid of these dogs. Permanently!"

Chapter Fourteen

Dare on the Air

DARE COULDN'T BELIEVE it when Mouse came trotting into the tree room. The two of them danced around the tree in a whirlwind of wagging tails and bouncing pompoms. This woke the puppies, who began to cry, so Dare settled down and nursed them while Mouse explained how he, Mew, and Ratter had come to the city. The puppies nursed for a short time, then began to cry again.

"My poor hungry puppies!" Dare licked their little heads. "If only I could make more milk for you."

"Is there a refrigerator in the building?" Mouse asked.

"Yes, but that doesn't do us any good. We need a human to open it."

"I know how to open refrigerators," said Mouse. "I saw Old Sam do it one night after everyone was in bed. You just push against the edge of the door with your head. He made me promise not to tell."

"Of all the nerve! Learning a trick like that and not sharing it with us," Dare said indignantly. "But you can't open it with your tiny head. I'll have to come with you. We'd better wait until lunchtime, when all the humans will be busy with their talking-to-the-cameras business."

At noon the camera barn lights blazed to life once more. No one noticed the two dogs enter the camera barn. The camera men had their backs to them, and the humans behind the desk couldn't see a thing with those bright lights shining in their eyes. Dare and Mew crept along the wall until they were safely out of the room.

The lunchroom was empty. Dare braced the top of her head against the edge of the refrigerator door and pushed. It was a small refrigerator, and the seal on the door was old and weak. It didn't take much effort to pry it open.

While Dare held the door open and watched for humans, Mouse jumped onto the lowest shelf, balancing his tiny paws on the thin metal bars. He tossed a bag down to Dare. She tore it open and devoured a mouth-watering tuna fish sandwich.

Footsteps approached as she was licking the last

traces of mayonnaise from the bag. Dare ducked behind the vending machine. Mouse spun around to jump down, but one of his front paws slipped between the metal bars of the shelf. When he tried to pull it free, his hind leg slipped through the bars as well, and the door swung shut with him still inside.

A man came into the room and sat down at one of the tables. He bent his head over a Styrofoam container and forked some noodles into his mouth. A woman walked over to the refrigerator and opened the door.

"Hey!"

"Hey what?" the noodle-eating man asked.

"Who ate my lunch?"

"Not me."

"It was so you. The bag is right by your table!"

The woman closed the door and began to argue with the noodle man. Dare growled softly in dismay. By the time these humans went back to work, Mouse would be a Chihuahua popsicle.

Another man and woman came in, both carrying paper bags.

"Where'd you go for lunch?" the woman asked the man.

"Taco Bell."

"*Yo quiero* Taco Bell!" the woman said in a funny voice.

The man put the bag on a table and pulled out some spicy-smelling food. "I never liked those Taco Bell commercials. That scary little Chihuahua gave me nightmares."

He opened the refrigerator and reached for a carton of milk. Mouse burst out from behind it, yapping hysterically. The man flew backwards as if a bomb had exploded in his face. Mouse bounced off his chest and hit the floor running, his little paws skittering on the tile. The humans abandoned their food and chased him out of the room. Dare wanted to go after them, but she couldn't risk getting caught and taken away from the puppies.

In the camera barn the humans were still talking to the cameras. Dare had almost reached the door to the tree room when a familiar bark caught her attention. Pierre! She whirled around, but Pierre was nowhere in sight. Wait, yes he was—he was in one of the TVs! Dare stared in amazement. The TV showed Pierre and Mew struggling in Beth's arms. Ratter, Sprout, and Cupcake were there too, clutched in Skid's arms.

The picture changed, showing the front of Beth's store with Skid's van stuck halfway through the window. Dare waited, but the dogs didn't come back. She returned to her puppies in a state of total bewilderment.

Mouse trotted into the tree room a few minutes

later. "That was a terrible raid. We never used to be this bad at stealing. I guess we're out of practice."

"Pierre and the others were in the TV!" she burst out.

"You're imagining things," he said. "Just like when my humans abandoned me and I kept thinking I saw them all over town."

The heavy lights that hung from the ceiling suddenly blazed like little suns. Behind the fake wall, a golden light threw fake sunlight through a fake window.

Dare ducked into her box and poked her head out. "Mouse! Where did you go?"

"Shhh!" He had leaped up into the tree to crouch on one of the branches.

"Why don't you hide in Pierre's box?"

"I don't like boxes."

"Oh, I forgot," Dare said softly. When Mouse's humans had abandoned him, they stuffed him into a little box and threw it out the window of their car as they drove away. He had been trapped in the box where it lay in the ditch until Dare came along and freed him. If Mr. Abram left any boxes on the floor, Mouse would chew them to bits. "Just to be safe," he'd say.

Several humans entered the room, two of them pushing cameras on pedestals. A blond woman went to sit down in one of the armchairs, then stopped.

"Where did the seat cushion go?"

"Craig said a coyote ate it," one of the camera humans said.

"I'll bet it was the Taco Bell Chihuahua," the other man said. "The one who knocked me down and stole Sandy's lunch."

"You know, if you guys keep drinking on the job, you're going to get fired," the woman warned.

Someone dragged a smaller chair into the room. The woman settled into it and pinned a small black object trailing a cord to her vest. She sipped a cup of coffee and stared at some papers in her hand while the two men aimed their cameras at her. The dogs had never seen such a fuss over a human sitting down for a cup of coffee.

"Hey, I know that woman," Dare said. "Mr. Abram watches her in the TV sometimes."

"That's impossible," Mouse scoffed from his tree perch. "The people in the TV aren't real. They have no scent."

Dare looked at the cameras. "It must be like a mirror. The people are real, but the TV is just a reflection."

"That's a pretty smart idea from a dog who keeps barking at herself in the mirror."

"I only did that *once*," said Dare indignantly. "It was dark, and I had a cold and couldn't smell."

Dare sensed movement out of the corner of her

eye. There was a window high up on one wall. Humans moved around behind the window, looking down at the room in a way that suggested they were supervising this coffee-drinking show.

A man came into the room and arranged several glass cases on the coffee table. He sat down as music poured out of ceiling speakers. One of the men rolled his camera toward the woman as if he meant to run her over with it, but he slowed to a halt as the music faded. The woman smiled and turned to the cameras.

"Welcome to *Prairie Focus*! I'm Brenda Millekin."

The two men peering into their cameras rudely ignored her.

"Our first guest is Rory Spracklin, an entomologist famous for his collection of exotic insects. Welcome to the show, Rory."

"Thank you, Brenda." The man folded his arms angrily. "Unfortunately, I can't show you my entire collection because most of my insects disappeared from your waiting room while I was in the bathroom."

Brenda turned pale. "You mean they're loose in the building?"

"It's a good thing you gave up your addiction to bugs, Mouse, or you'd be going crazy right now," Dare said, looking at the fat, colorful beetles in the man's glass cases.

Mouse burped.

Over the next hour, more humans came into the room to sit down next to the woman and chat with her. One woman showed Brenda how to paint colors on her face. A man demonstrated how to make little animals out of paper. It was all terribly boring, and Mouse soon dozed off, draped across his tree branch. Dare cleaned the puppies and worried about Pierre and the others. She wasn't sure how their reflections had gotten into the TV, but one thing was certain. That awful Beth had taken them prisoner, and there was no one to rescue them.

Unless...

She stuck her head out of the box and looked at the cameras. Brenda bid the last guest farewell, then sat down and waited for the music to stop so she could start talking to the cameras again.

"You know, if Mr. Abram can see *her*..." Dare fell into a thoughtful silence.

"We end our program on a sad note," the woman said, tilting her head at a sorrowful angle, like Old Sam begging for scraps at the dinner table. "Earlier this year, a brave group of homeless dogs gave up their freedom to save the life of a Silvertree man. In his gratitude, Peter Abram adopted those dogs. Tragically, those dogs have gone missing. Peter Abram is heartbroken over the loss of the dogs. Kevin Blake was in Silvertree earlier today speaking with Mr. Abram."

"Tape is rolling, we're clear," announced one of the men behind the cameras. Brenda sat back in her chair and sipped her coffee, shuffling through the papers in her hand.

Mouse, peeking through the branches of the tree, let out a startled squeak. "We're in the TV!"

Close to one of the cameras a TV on a stand had been turned so Brenda could see it. The screen showed Old Sam, Pierre, Dare, Mew, and Mouse playing in the snow in the Silvertree Park. Dare remembered that day. Mr. Abram had brought his camera along.

All at once Mr. Abram's wistful voice came out of the speakers. "Mitzy and Mouse disappeared from my house just yesterday. They must have run away to look for Pierre and Dare. If anyone has found them, please return them to their home. They mean the world to me."

Mouse nearly fell out of the tree and Dare looked wildly around, but there was no sign or scent of Mr. Abram. The people in the room carried on idle conversation as if they couldn't even hear Mr. Abram talking to them.

One of the men behind the cameras said, "We're back on the air in five...four...three...two..."

Mr. Abram's voice stopped and Brenda spoke to the camera again. "Anyone with information regarding the missing dogs should contact the local—"

119

She got no farther than that, for with a short dash and a long leap, Dare was on top of the coffee table, scattering papers everywhere. The cup went flying, spilling coffee onto the white carpet. Dare looked at the cameras and barked.

Brenda screamed and leaped to her feet. The two men smashed their cameras together as they scrambled to focus on the small dog. Someone in the room above yelled, "Stop screaming into your microphone!"

"Dare!" Mouse cried. "What are you doing? Mr. Abram isn't here. It's just one of those reflections."

"I know what I'm doing!" Dare ran under the tree and jumped into her box with the puppies. When the man who had let Mouse out of the refrigerator crawled under the tree and reached for Dare's box, Mouse leaped out of the tree with an explosion of shrill barks. The man screamed and ran out of the room.

"It's all right," Dare said. "Let them see the puppies!"

The humans pulled the box out from under the tree and opened it.

"Awww!" they crooned when they saw Dare curled around her puppies.

Mouse paced anxiously, jumping out of reach when the humans tried to pet him. "They'll take us to the animal shelter!"

"No, they won't," Dare said. "I never thought I'd say this, but we're going to have to trust the humans. They're our only hope of getting all of us home in one piece!"

Chapter Fifteen

Prairie Pursuit

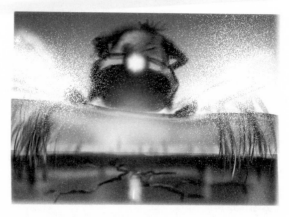

AS THE HOURS PASSED, the noise above slowly faded away. Pierre paced his cage, frantic with worry. There was no way to escape. Beth certainly wouldn't fall for any more of his tricks. And what about Dare and their poor hungry puppies? Would he ever see them again?

Beth and Skid came down the stairs. Beth handed Skid a slip of paper.

"Here's the address of a guy in Medicine Hat. He said he'd give me five hundred dollars for the purebreds, no questions asked."

"What about the two mongrels?" asked Skid.

"Naw, he doesn't want them. Just dump them into a trashcan along the highway."

Beth and Skid pulled the dogs out of their cages. Just as Beth lifted Pierre and Mew into her arms, Mew puffed out her fur and let out her fiercest hiss. Beth screamed and dropped the two dogs. At the same time, Ratter reached up and nipped Skid's nose. He, too, tumbled to the floor, along with Cupcake and Sprout. The dogs were up the stairs in an instant. The humans had taped plastic over the broken window, but Pierre burst right through it.

The dogs ran down the sidewalk as fast as their legs would carry them. Beth and Skid jumped into the badly dented van and roared after them. Pierre gasped in relief when they reached the park. The van couldn't follow them here. Beth and Skid jumped out and chased after them, but Pierre just snorted in contempt. As if any human on foot could keep up with a dog!

A few minutes later, he wasn't feeling so cocky. Hunger and the long distance they had traveled today had weakened Pierre, Mew, and Ratter. Sprout was already half frozen, and Cupcake's little legs were no match for the long legs of the humans. Beth and Skid were gaining on them. The dogs managed to lose them among the snow sculptures, but by the time they reached the edge of the park, the two humans had caught sight of them again.

Beth, puffing loudly, fell behind as they chased the dogs across the fields, but Skid was right behind them when they slipped under the fence of the cow pasture. Both of his ears and his nose were swollen from being nipped, giving him a frightful appearance.

Pierre barked as loudly as he could, then gasped, "Hide in the hay!"

The dogs burrowed into the loose hay the cows had pulled from their big round bale. As Skid leaned down to dig them out, he heard a deep, angry bark. It was the farm dog. Skid tried to climb the hay bale, but it was too slippery, so he climbed one of the cows. The cow bolted across the pasture with Skid clinging to her back and the Chow cross nipping at Skid's boots.

"Not far now," Pierre encouraged the exhausted dogs as they left the pasture. "See the blinking tower and the brick building? That's where—"

A distant buzzing noise caught his attention. He looked over his shoulder. A man on a snowmobile zoomed across the prairie, and behind him rode Beth. They caught sight of the dogs and swerved toward them.

"Run!" Pierre cried, though he knew it was hopeless. They would never get to the TV building before the snowmobile caught up to them.

Then he remembered the night of the blizzard and the feel of slippery ice beneath his paws. He led the dogs into a depression among the low prairie hills. Here he sat down, panting. The other dogs, thinking he had given up, whimpered in fear. The snowmobile roared toward them, slowing as it approached. Beth gave them a nasty grin and the driver gave them a friendly one, probably thinking he was doing them a favor by reuniting them with their owner.

Suddenly, the snowmobile's nose dipped down and the vehicle jolted to a stop. It had broken through the ice of the shallow pond hidden beneath the snow. Beth and the driver scrambled off and backed away, cursing. Pierre grinned as only a poodle can grin and led his little pack away from the pond.

But Beth still hadn't given up on them. Onward she came, gasping for breath but slowly catching up to them.

"...get rid of you...if it's the last thing I do," she wheezed.

Pierre's legs were shaking with exhaustion, and poor little Cupcake would have collapsed if not for Ratter nudging her along.

But they made it! They were at the TV building. Pierre tottered toward the vent, then fell back in dismay. The humans had discovered the loose cover and put it back in place. He jumped up and hooked his claws into the mesh, but it didn't budge.

Too tired to run, the dogs huddled together

against the brick wall as Beth loomed over them. She reached for them—

—and a streak of black and white feathers swooped out of the sky, scraping Beth's head with its claws. Beth screamed and flailed her arms.

"Go to the front door, little dogs!" The magpie turned and plummeted down for another pass at Beth's head. "You'll find someone there who will be very happy to see you!"

"Thanks, Pica!" The dogs staggered around the corner of the building. A man stood there, smoking a cigarette with nervous little puffs. Sprout stumbled over to him, shivering with cold and drooling with exhaustion. The man stared at the hairless little dog with the wild bursts of fur on his head and paws.

"The Chihuahua's mutating!" he yelled, and tore into the building, slamming the door behind him.

"He didn't look very happy to see us," Mew said.

The dogs crossed over to the next corner. Pierre peered around it, but his view was blocked by snowy bushes.

A suffocating darkness fell over him. He felt himself and the others swept up into a pair of strong arms. He struggled wildly and managed to free his head. It was Beth who held him. She had thrown her coat over the dogs.

"Forget selling you. You're all going into the river, you crazy dogs!" She shook the coat menacingly.

Then she screamed. A small red dog had shot across the parking lot and was attacking her ankles.

"Dare!" Pierre cried.

"And Mouse!" cried the fierce little Chihuahua who joined the attack. Pica sailed by and dropped a cigarette on Beth's head.

Beth dropped the dogs and kicked wildly at Dare and Mouse while flapping her arms and shaking her head. She looked like she was doing some kind of crazy dance.

"Stop that at once!" cried a familiar voice. "How dare you try to hurt my dogs?"

Pierre thought he must be dreaming. Surely that couldn't be Mr. Abram hurrying across the parking lot, shaking his cane at Beth? Only when his nose caught the scent of tweed and piney soap and breakfast sausages did he believe what his eyes were telling him.

"They're my dogs," Beth shouted.

"They most certainly are not!"

"You stole them, didn't you?" said the blond woman next to Mr. Abram. Pierre recognized her. Mr. Abram often watched her in the TV after lunch. She picked up Sprout, who had pressed himself against her leg, trying to get warm. "I recognize these dogs from the van crash story we ran at noon. The SPCA told us someone has been stealing little dogs from small towns around the province. One of those dogs was a Chinese crested!"

Pierre no longer cared about Beth. He and Mew flew into Mr. Abram's arms. Dare and Mouse squeezed in between them, happily licking everyone within reach. Cupcake tried to join them but quickly scooted away when Dare growled at her.

"It's no use," Cupcake said to Ratter. "We're just going to have to find our own human."

"We?" Ratter said.

"I've decided Pierre's not my mate anymore," she said. "You are."

"What?" Ratter spluttered. "I don't want no sissy little poodle for a mate!"

"That blond woman looks just right for us. Come on, let's go get ourselves adopted."

Dare was trying to explain something about Mr.

Abram seeing them in a TV, but Pierre had only one concern. "Where are the puppies? Are they all right?"

Dare nudged Mr. Abram's thick tweed coat. Mr. Abram opened the top of the coat. There, cuddled warmly against his chest, were their two puppies.

"My dear Pierre!" Mr. Abram said. "What a lovely family you have."

Chapter Sixteen
TV Dogs

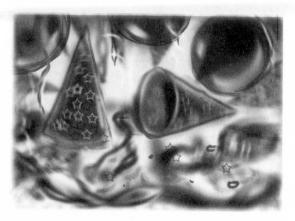

"LOOK, we're in the TV again!" Mew exclaimed. "And so is Mr. Abram."

Mr. Abram was staying up late to watch TV, and the dogs were sharing the couch with him. For some reason, Mr. Abram had put little pointy hats on the dogs, even Old Sam. They were feeling too content to protest this example of human strangeness.

The only one who had anything to complain about was Dare. Mr. Abram had washed away all the city scents she had collected.

"I love Mr. Abram, but he has no appreciation for a fine scent," she grumbled.

"Our most miraculous story of the year took place just two weeks ago," the blond woman in the

TV was saying. It was Brenda, who liked to drink coffee and talk to cameras. "I'm sure you all remember the story of the Silvertree Dogs."

The TV showed Brenda talking with Mr. Abram. Their conversation was interspersed with pictures of the dogs at the TV building, and pictures of Beth and Skid in a police car. There were many shots of the puppies. Pierre glanced over at his son and daughter, proud of how much they had grown. Their eyes were open, and they were doing their best to climb out of their kitchen pen and explore, although with two watchful parents and three puppysitters, it wouldn't be easy.

"Brenda says viewers have been calling in, accusing the TV station of kidnapping you just to create a news story," Mr. Abram told the dogs.

"We at CKPD-TV wish all of you a happy new year," Brenda said. "And keep those dogs of yours safely at home this year. I know I will!"

A ragged white terrier and a tiny apricot poodle jumped into her lap and peered alertly into the camera. Brenda gave her two new dogs a hug.

The doorbell rang. The dogs barked in case Mr. Abram hadn't noticed.

Mr. Abram gave them an apologetic glance as he went to the door. "I invited him over to show there are no hard feelings. He feels terrible about what happened to you."

Mr. Abram opened the door and Calloway staggered in.

"Sorry I'm late, Abram, I got hung up at the ranch. Fox got one of my birds—but that won't be a problem much longer."

He opened his arms and a pair of enormous puppies dropped to the floor. Barking thunderously, they galloped around the living room, knocking over a rocking chair and the coffee table. A bowl of popcorn flew all over the room. One of the giant puppies attempted to sniff noses with Pierre but misjudged the distance and knocked him off the couch.

"Great Dane–collie crosses!" Calloway shouted. "Just picked them up today. With those two guarding my livestock, I'll never have to worry about predators again. I figured you could help me train them. I don't know much about dogs. Hey, your little Chihuahua just fainted."

"This is your fault," Old Sam said to Pierre and Dare. "You're the ones who brought Titan and Sheba together."

Mr. Abram handed Calloway a pointy hat. "You're just in time, Mr. Calloway."

In the TV, humans were chanting, "Four... three...two...one...Happy New Year!"

Mr. Abram and Calloway blew on little pink tubes that whistled and shot out a roll of paper.

Mew snapped Calloway's away from him and shredded it, in case it was some sort of weapon.

"Well, my dears, we've made it through another year," Mr. Abram said. "I hope this one will hold a little less adventure for you than the last."

Calloway, looking at the nine dogs, just shook his head and laughed.

THE END

About the Author

Because of chronic asthma, Glenda Goertzen spent much of her childhood in bed, reading and writing stories. She wrote her first novel in grade nine, a science fiction adventure for children. Her English teacher urged her to enter it in a contest. Although Glenda didn't win, the experience encouraged her to write novels throughout high school. One of those novels was *The Prairie Dogs*, inspired by stray dogs she had known and by the imaginary adventures of her favorite toy as a child, a stuffed poodle named Pooch.

Glenda wrote *The Prairie Dogs* and *City Dogs* to entertain children who love animals, but she also wanted to describe Canada's natural environment in a way children can relate to, through the eyes of an inquisitive outsider, a creature who lives through his senses. The beauty and adventure of the Canadian prairie are best appreciated at ground level, and who better to describe them than a small dog?